Doctor Harris

Clara Ann Simons

Doctor Harris

Clara Ann Simons

Copyright © 2023 by Clara Ann Simons.

All Rights Reserved.

Registered on Oct. 11/2023

All rights reserved. No part of this material may be reproduced in any form or by any means without the express permission of the author. This includes, but is not limited to, reprints, excerpts, photocopying, recording, or any other means of reproduction, including electronic means.

All characters, situations between them and events appearing in the book are entirely fictitious. Any resemblance to persons, living or dead, or events is purely coincidental.

The cover is for illustrative purposes, any person appearing is a model and bears no relation whatsoever to the content of the book, its author, or any of the main characters.

The book contains some explicit sex scenes.

For more information, or if you want to know about new publications, please contact us via email at claraannsimons@gmail.com

Index

CHAPTER 1	5
CHAPTER 2	12
CHAPTER 3	18
CHAPTER 4	24
CHAPTER 5	30
CHAPTER 6	38
CHAPTER 7	48
CHAPTER 8	57
CHAPTER 9	65
CHAPTER 10	73
CHAPTER 11	82
CHAPTER 12	94

CHAPTER 13	**102**
CHAPTER 14	**112**
CHAPTER 15	**119**
CHAPTER 16	**130**
CHAPTER 17	**140**
CHAPTER 18	**150**
EPILOG	**159**
OTHER BOOKS BY THE SAME AUTHOR	**165**

Chapter 1

The heart of Manhattan's Watson Memorial Hospital is a three-ring circus. Doctors bark orders, nurses scurry between rooms, and orderlies wheel patients through the organized chaos. Everyone is focused on their own act of pessimism or hope.

Around me, a cacophony of beeps, buzzes, and distant voices whisper in my ears. The sharp scent of antiseptic stings my nose, mingling with the lavender perfume I dabbed on this morning in a vain attempt to mask the hospital smells.

Strangely, this controlled chaos feels like a home away from home. My sanctuary from the stresses of the outside world.

I stroll down the fluorescent-lit hall, familiar now in my second year of residency. Some offer a wave or tired smile as I pass. A few take the time to mutter a brief "Good morning, Doctor," their minds already focused on the patients and tasks ahead.

"Well, well, if it isn't Doctor Arya Kumari, slumming it in this part of the hospital," I joke over my shoulder to the tough-looking woman in blue scrubs behind me.

"We miss you up in cardiac surgery, you know." She winks, her huge brown eyes crinkling with warmth despite the cocky grin. "Just in case you decide to choose a specialty. The new residents just don't have your spark."

I snort, rolling my eyes dramatically. "Is that your professional medical opinion, Doctor?"

Working with Dr. Kumari last year was an experience like no other. She just transferred here from LA's Collins Memorial with her wife, adopted kid, scruffy dog, and two cats in tow, ready to take on the New York hospital scene.

Arya Kumari is the opposite of your typical prestigious cardiac surgeon. Raised in the slums of LA by Indian immigrant parents, she clawed her way up from nothing to follow her passion for medicine.

She looks more back-alley brawler than a top medical school-educated doctor, with her pierced eyebrow and the faint shadow of a tear-drop tattoo peeking above her collar. She swears every other word without thought. But behind the brash exterior lies a heart of gold.

Easily the most helpful doctor I've worked with, along with Ines Torres. Though Ines doesn't really count, since her girlfriend also happens to be my best friend from college and former roommate.

"Oh, and your jackass of a boss is looking for you," Arya calls out as I continue down the hall.

I let out an exaggerated groan, eliciting a chuckle from her. Just another day at the office.

The smile evaporates from my lips as I see my boss striding toward me. His icy blue eyes and neatly trimmed silver temples give him an air of arrogance. Over six feet tall and carrying extra weight around his middle, he lumbers toward me with less grace than he'd like. With his intimidating presence, he reminds me of a silverback gorilla dressed in a white coat.

"Good morning, Rachel," he purrs, stroking my left arm. It's a habit I once tolerated but now makes me recoil. "How's the universe treating you this fine Monday morning?" His bleached-white veneer flashes in a forced grin.

"Oh, surviving," I reply casually with a noncommittal shrug.

"And how was your weekend?" He peers down at me over his glasses. "Meet anyone special lately?"

Like clockwork, the same invasive question every Monday. Never forgotten. Constantly prodding me about my personal life and dating prospects as if I'd disclose those details to him.

"Can't complain," I say dryly.

"You're looking radiant today, by the way. New haircut?"

Arya swears my boss watches too many medical dramas and fancies himself the protagonist, wooing all the young nurses and residents. The worst part is he believes in his own delusion. He can't seem to stop hitting on any woman under forty who crosses his path.

"Oh, and my wife is out of town for a few days on business," he adds casually. "Care to grab a drink after work sometime this week?" He arches an eyebrow, grinning expectantly.

I fight the urge to vomit right there in the hallway. "I have patients to see, Richard," I reply evenly, struggling to rein in my disgust.

I quicken my pace to pull away, feeling his eyes follow me for a moment.

"Think about it. Offer's open if you change your mind." He calls after me with unearned familiarity. "We'd have fun."

I stay silent, not trusting myself to reply professionally. Just two more months under his supervision in this program. I'll choose another specialty if it means avoiding working beside him in the future. Doesn't help that his father-in-law sits on the hospital's board of directors.

Soon, his inappropriate proposition fades into the distance behind me. I begin my morning rounds checking on patients, starting with Mr. Johnson in room 402. At seventy years old, he's recovering well from an aortic valve replacement surgery last week. A perpetually cheerful and optimistic man, I can't help but smile when I see his name on my patient list for the day. There are some people you just root for a little harder.

In the next room over, 403, a little girl's innocent laughter reaches my ears. Six-year-old Emma sits propped up in her hospital bed, surrounded by a wall of get-well toys and balloons. She grins up at me as I enter, her eyes sparkling despite the IV needled into her arm.

"Rachel!" Emma calls out as I enter her room. "I made you a picture. It's you!" She hands me a crayon drawing of what looks like a stick figure doctor caring for a smaller stick figure patient in a bed.

"Well, would you look at this masterpiece! This is fridge door gallery material, for sure. Should we put it in a museum instead?"

Emma giggles, a grin lighting up her face despite her missing front teeth. Her smile could outshine the sun itself. My heart inflates like a hot air balloon, reminding me why I chose this career, even on the hard days.

"On your fridge!" she declares.

"Then that's where it will go. I'll bring you a photo tomorrow so you can see it in its new home." I smile back as I check her vitals one last time before moving on.

I take a deep breath as I leave Emma's room, bracing myself for the next visit. Claudia, a 45-year-old woman, wages a relentless battle for her life behind the next door. I enter quietly, taking in her fragile form under the thin blanket. Life and death, side by side.

"Good morning," I whisper, clasping her slender hand. "How are you feeling today?"

She opens her eyes slowly, pain etched on her gaunt face. "I've had better days, Dr. Harris. The pain is bad today." Her voice is barely a whisper.

"I'm sorry to hear that, Claudia. Let's increase your medication a bit to help ease it. Does that sound alright?" I fluff her pillow gently.

She gives a small nod, unable to expend the energy to respond. We can only watch helplessly as her light continues to dim before our eyes.

"Hit the call button if you need anything at all. Someone will come right away," I remind her.

I glance at my watch. It's almost time for a short break on this nonstop day. Time flies in this job, for better or worse.

Chapter 2

My mind replays the last worrisome patient as I head back to the break room for a much-needed respite. Then the emergency pager blares, jolting me like a lightning strike. Adrenaline courses through my veins.

"Major car accident coming in. Woman named Natalie Fey, critical condition," my boss announces in his usual monotone, not even glancing up from his chart.

His lack of emotion when announcing critical cases always strikes me. I can't decide if he's become utterly desensitized over the years or internalizes his feelings too deeply after decades in medicine. Either way, his detached demeanor never wavers, not even a fraction.

When I was an intern in cardiac surgery, Dr. Arya Kumari kept her cool in the OR even during tense open heart operations. But afterward, you could see each patient affected her. Losing one completely devastated her. Richard seems to feel nothing at all.

I rush after him down the fluorescent-lit hallway, heart racing, mentally preparing to do everything humanly possible to save this woman coming to us clinging to life. Just another adrenaline-filled day as a resident in the ER.

My heart pounds erratically, echoing in my ears as we push through the double doors into the chaotic emergency room.

"What's the situation?" Richard barks at the team swarming around the gurney.

"Female, thirty-two. ID confirms name as Natalie Fey. Major car accident based on paramedic report. Trouble breathing and seizures in the ambulance. That's all we know for now," a nurse briefs us urgently.

Richard nods slowly, almost solemnly, listening to the rapid-fire medical terms and vital signs being called out as the team evaluates her. I can't help but glance at Natalie's broken body. She looks so vulnerable and small, lying there, battered and bloody, dark hair matted to her forehead. My stomach twists.

"We're going to need to intubate to stabilize her," Richard announces.

"Are you sure that's necessary already?" I question without thinking.

Richard glares at me, his blue eyes icy. "Did I ask your opinion, Dr. Harris?" he snaps, suddenly abrasive. A stark contrast to his usual flirtatious tone with me.

I raise my hands in surrender, not wanting to challenge my boss with everyone watching.

I agree about the likely brain inflammation from trauma, but inducing a coma seems overly aggressive without further tests. From what I've seen, it often leads to more extended ICU stays and other risks associated with ventilation. Maybe a lighter sedation could work, but I won't question an experienced doctor's call.

We leap into action without a second to spare, carefully inserting the endotracheal tube. The room buzzes with tension, all of us holding our breath. Time seems frozen.

"She's stable. Let's move her to the ICU," Richard announces, breaking the spell.

Our work here is done. Now, we wait for her to be transferred to intensive care for the most critical phase of recovery. If all goes well, I may see Natalie again in a few days before she's moved to a regular room.

Richard nudges my shoulder, jolting me from my thoughts. "Follow me!"

I trail him down the sterile hallway, unsure if he plans to scold me for speaking out earlier.

But I can't shake Natalie's image from my mind. Despite the bruising, she was strikingly beautiful — toned figure without an ounce of fat, flawless. She must spend endless hours sculpting that body in the gym.

"What's the plan for her from here?" I ask.

Richard's brow furrows in confusion. "What do you mean?"

"Natalie, the car crash victim. Isn't that what you wanted to discuss?"

"Oh, no. I just wanted to confirm our drinks tonight," he replies casually.

I must fight the urge to slap that smug grin off his face. A wave of rage courses through me. We just put a woman in a medically induced coma with a brain bleed. She may have permanent damage, if she even survives. And this pompous jackass only cares about cheating on his wife.

"I don't think that's appropriate, Richard," I reply through gritted teeth, struggling to stay professional.

He shrugs. "Suit yourself. But the offer stands if you change your mind." He winks before sauntering off, leaving me fuming in the hallway.

How did a pompous jerk like Richard, obsessed with any woman young enough to be his daughter, get appointed head of the ER? Oh, right, daddy-in-law pulling strings on the hospital board. Classic nepotism.

"They'll run more tests, Rachel. Once we know more, we can properly treat her. She's not our concern now," he shrugs as if her life doesn't matter in the least.

"Would it have been so hard to say that upfront?" I ask, straining to stay professional.

Richard gives me an icy stare that could freeze hell itself. "If you weren't so hot, I would've transferred you to another department by now," he spits out scornfully.

"You know you can't talk to me like that, right?"

"But you won't say anything to anyone, will you?" he whispers, leaning in until his face is just inches from mine.

I swallow hard, too stunned to respond. My breathing quickens, and he knows he's won this round. That smug grin returns as he turns on his heel and saunters away.

"I'll update you if anything changes," he calls over his shoulder. "Oh, and drinks tonight...your loss. You're not the only hot resident, you know. That attitude won't earn you a permanent ER spot."

"Pompous jackass," I mutter under my breath once he's out of earshot.

Chapter 3

The harsh beep of my pager pierces the quiet, startling me from my brief respite. We only use them for true emergencies now, so I know it must be serious.

"Harris, get down to the ICU and check on the woman in a coma. I'll be there shortly," reads Richard's message. My frustratingly charming boss.

I drag my feet down the long, dimly lit hospital corridor toward the intensive care unit where Natalie Fey lies motionless. The too-sterile scent of antiseptic hits me as soon as I step through the double doors, both reassuring and terrifying at the same time.

As I approach Natalie's bedside, I take in her utterly still form under the stark white sheets, the harsh fluorescent lights buzzing overhead, the steady beeps and whirs of machinery.

The ICU is a world unto itself — a world governed by monitors emitting frightening alarms. One of cautious conversations spoken in hushed whispers. A world that pulses with tense energy during visiting hours as families keep silent vigils, praying for any small sign of hope.

Doctor Harris

I let out a long, slow breath as I sink into the chair beside Natalie's bed, her chart in hand. She's still intubated, nestled into a tangled mess of wires and tubes connecting her fragile body to the imposing machines around us. She looks almost like a mermaid caught in a fisherman's net.

The heart rate monitor blinks an eerie, endless green, faithfully tracking each beat of her heart. It's a chilling reminder that beneath the exterior stillness required for her medically-induced coma, life continues fighting relentlessly on.

I catch myself smiling softly as I gently brush a stray strand of dark hair off her battered forehead. The caked blood may be gone, but angry bruises and cuts remain.

As I study her face, I can't help but wonder about her life before the terrible accident landed her here. One of the nurses mentioned no emergency contacts were listed for her. No friends or family have come to visit. It must be so painfully lonely — waking up alone from a coma, with no familiar loved ones by your side.

"Natalie," I find myself whispering her name softly, as if, on some level, she can still hear me.

I'm not sure why I reach out to lightly squeeze her hand, my thumb absently caressing her soft skin. Maybe it's some instinctive attempt to offer her strength and comfort as she clings to life. And for a fleeting moment, I can almost imagine the sound of her laugh.

I wish someone who truly cared was here holding her hand, talking to her, urging her to keep fighting. That's real love — being steadfastly by their side even when the light seems to fade. Offering words of hope and comfort even when your own voice shakes with fear.

So, I talk. I tell her a silly story of the day's happenings around the hospital. Pointless ramblings since she can't actually hear, but it makes me feel a little better.

Just then, Richard comes sweeping into the ICU, his white lab coat billowing around him like a superhero cape. His Cheshire cat grin means he must be in a good mood, but my stomach sinks at the sight of him.

"Well, well, let's see how Ms. Natalie Fey is doing today," he announces brightly.

"No changes. Vitals remain stable," I report flatly, avoiding eye contact.

I respond in the most professional way possible, without even looking him in the eye.

He comes over and circles my waist slyly, making sure the ICU nurses can't see what he's doing.

"Did you change your mind about tonight?" he whispers, pretending to check the patient's vitals.

I grit my teeth and get up abruptly with the excuse of adjusting the IV drip. My job is to treat patients, to learn from the doctors who supervise my work on each rotation, not to sleep with them.

For a few moments, I ponder confronting him, even talking to the HR department. At the very least, I'd like to ask him why he keeps insisting on pushing the envelope in the vain hope that I'll change my mind, when I'm never going to.

"You haven't answered me," he insists, and I can't take it any longer.

"Why do you keep trying with me when I've already told you a million times no? Not to mention that you're married," I remind my boss, giving him my fiercest look.

"My marriage is in the shit, Rachel. I'd like to get to know you better, you know, see if we're compatible," he adds with a wink that's meant to be seductive, though it makes me want to puke in his pants.

"And what does your wife think about that?"

"I guess she's too busy with her yoga instructor," he replies with a shrug.

It would almost be funny if it weren't such a strange situation. In the end, Arya will be right, and this man has escaped from a doctor's soap opera.

"What about you, Rachel? You never answer me why you don't have a boyfriend," his tone turns my stomach once again.

I take a deep breath and tremble with rage, wishing I could slap him in the face.

"Did I hit a nerve? With that body of yours, aren't you any good in bed?"

I clench my fists, wishing I could stick a scalpel in his eye, but violence wouldn't solve much, so I try to keep my composure.

"That can't be it, can it?" Richard asks when he sees that I've become very tense.

"Get out of here, Richard, please," I ask as calmly as I can. "I'll keep checking Natalie's vitals."

"Oh, is that Natalie now?" he asks in surprise.

"Please, Richard, I'm only going to ask you one more time," I sigh.

My boss frowns and reluctantly hands me the medical chart. He practically slams it against my chest. Then he spins on his heel and leaves the room, but not before mumbling a *"cock teasing slut"* between his teeth, loud enough for me to hear perfectly.

Deep down, he knows a scandal wouldn't be good for either of us. Even if it's his word against mine and I have everything to lose thanks to his contacts, suspicion would float in the air.

And without Richard in the room, a strange peace comes over me. I return to sit by Natalie's bedside, captivated by her beauty as she sleeps.

For some reason, the Brothers Grimm's tale of Sleeping Beauty comes back to me. My grandmother used to read it to me as a child, and I imagine Natalie waking up to the kiss of a prince. Or, in this case, a princess.

Chapter 4

Monday morning. I open my eyes only to have them fall shut again. I'm exhausted. The past week has been crushing: long shifts at the hospital, paperwork piled on by my boss. It's like Richard is punishing me for refusing to have dinner with him. Some days, the only thing keeping me going is Natalie.

I visit her whenever I can. I've sat by her bedside this past week, talking to her even though she can't respond. It's become an escape, a one-sided conversation where I tell her about my life. I know she likely can't hear me, but one of the ICU doctors says it certainly won't hurt.

On Saturday night, I found myself opening up, telling her things I've never shared. My childhood dreams of fairy tales, my girlhood longing for a prince charming that I now hope will be a princess. How I'd get lost in fantasy romance novels in high school.

Looking at Natalie, so peaceful in her bed, I wondered if she could be the happy ending I've always imagined. She seems kind and affectionate, no wedding ring or tan line. And now that the bruises are fading, she really is beautiful.

For some reason, I told her about my parents' marriage — bound by routine more than love or passion. I promised her I'd fight with everything I have not to end up like them. I want a woman who attracts me but also someone I can trust. A partner who will care for me as much as I care for her. Someone who makes me feel safe and loved. That matters more to me than looks. I want a book romance.

The more time I spend with Natalie, the more I start to believe she could be that person. The one I've been waiting for. The woman I could build my dream with.

Arya says I'm crazy. "That's really disturbing, dumbass," she told me. Maybe she's right, but I can't help seeing Natalie that way.

"You know, yesterday was a shitshow at the hospital, back to back emergencies. And Richard's constant attempts to get in my pants don't help. I try to avoid him, but he's my boss and has a lot of power here," I explain as if she can understand.

The steady beep of the heart monitor has become as familiar as my own heartbeat. Sometimes, I imagine she's just sleeping. I dream that she'll open her eyes at any moment, and I'll lose myself in them.

"I googled you yesterday," I confess in a hushed voice as if it were our most intimate secret. "I know I shouldn't have, but I couldn't resist. With your toned body, I thought you could be a pro athlete. I never guessed you were a dancer. Then, I spent hours watching your YouTube videos. Seeing you dance on Broadway was the most beautiful thing I've ever seen. I hope one day I can watch you in person," I whisper, squeezing her hand in mine.

I smile remembering those videos, her graceful movements, her beauty. It's an image seared into my memory. I sit a while longer, telling her my fears and frustrations, my doubts about choosing a medical specialty. Her stillness and our one-sided chats are a balm for my stress.

***

"I'm starting to worry about you and this woman in a coma," Arya whispers in my ear.

"Are you sure your wife is okay with this?" I ask for the hundredth time.

According to Arya, we have what she calls an asexual polyamorous relationship. In practice, we cuddle in the break room during shared shifts, nothing more than pecks on the neck or cheek. But it makes me uncomfortable that she's married.

"I told you, Patricia trusts me completely. We met in LA, and I already had this thing going with Laura Park. There's nothing wrong with affection. Everyone needs it," she assures me.

"Are you jealous of the coma woman?" I ask.

"No, fuck. You're an idiot. What kind of question is that?" she snaps, rolling her eyes.

"Then what is it?"

"I don't know, it's disturbing. You visit her every day. I think you're falling in love with her."

"I'm not falling in love." I protest.

"Fuck, no. Don't be a jerk. You're totally hung up on that woman. I mean, I admit she's hot and all, but fuck, Rachel, she's in a coma."

"I only talk to her," I complain.

"Do you have any fantasies?"

"Arya! I'm not going to answer that kind of nonsense," I assure her, turning on the bed to lose myself in her huge black eyes.

"Fuck, it's much worse than I imagined," she jokes, rolling her eyes.

"You're such an idiot!"

"I want details." Arya teases.

"You're so silly. And you're crazy, but you're one of the few people I can talk to in this hospital."

***

"Yesterday, I imagined you were completely cured, and we went to Central Park together," I tell Natalie, lowering my voice and glancing around to make sure no one overhears. "It was sunset, and we strolled hand-in-hand along the paths, leaving the city noise behind."

I pause as an ICU nurse approaches to check the monitors, something she's probably done a million times. To her, Natalie is just another patient, a number.

"We spread a blanket on the grass," I go on, "and you pulled out delicious sandwiches and a bottle of white wine. We laughed so much. As we ate, the sky transformed into vibrant pinks and oranges, and soon, the first stars appeared. We kissed, your hair tickling my neck."

I stop, realizing I'm stroking her cheek. I take a deep breath, try to compose myself. As I described it, the scene felt so real I was scared.

For a moment, the world disappeared, and it was just Natalie and me on a romantic date existing only in my imagination. Yet I swear I could feel the warmth of her body curled against mine.

"I combed my fingers through your hair. You glanced up with such tenderness. My heart nearly stopped when you took my hand and kissed it. Slowly, evening fell around us, and the darkness witnessed a perfect moment."

Damn, maybe Arya is right, and I'm becoming obsessed with this woman.

Chapter 5

I pry one eye open with a groan, fumbling to silence the offensive noise of my morning alarm. As the fog of sleep clears, I'm reminded it's Monday yet again. But then thoughts of Natalie push their way forward, and the day of the week suddenly loses importance.

I was told Natalie's condition has improved tremendously. A nurse mentioned they'll be taking her off the ventilator and stopping sedation this week, the crucial steps to bring her out of the coma. I'm hopeful the process goes smoothly so we can finally meet face-to-face.

I find myself picturing her alert, those striking eyes meeting mine, and I wonder how having an actual conversation with her will feel. Surreal doesn't begin to describe it.

After a rushed shower, I gulp down coffee, lost in daydreams about our impending encounter. The shrill beep of my watch alerts me it's time to head to the hospital, where my grumpy boss, Richard, awaits. The man is more inconvenient than a busted clock, always dispatching me on endless patient rounds at the most inopportune times.

By eleven o'clock, I'm finally free of Richard's demands for a small while and have a break. I make my way to the hospital's cafeteria, craving a caffeine fix. Arya is already parked in our usual corner table, two steaming mugs and a croissant oozing butter in front of her.

"Took you long enough, dumbass," she greets me bluntly in typical Arya fashion. Her brash demeanor would seem off-putting to anyone else, but I know she's a secret softie at heart.

"Not my fault. Try dealing with Mr. Ferguson in 315. The man's demands rival a president's," I shoot back with an exaggerated eye roll.

Arya cackles at this, nearly knocking over her mug as she leans forward conspiratorially.

"Listen to this," she says, eyes sparkling devilishly. "I'm elbow-deep in this guy's gallbladder, routine procedure, when 'Dance Monkey' suddenly blasts over the OR speakers."

"No way!" I sputter, barely avoiding a spit-take.

She launches into a dramatic re-telling, flailing her arms as she imitates the flustered anesthesiologist scrambling to cut the music. Soon, we're both laughing so hard that tears roll down our cheeks. Doctors at nearby tables shake their heads and chuckle, well-accustomed to our antics. When Arya spins one of her wild tales, the rest of the world fades away.

"You're terrible! Poor guy."

"Poor guy? I almost started dancing with the patient's guts. I love that song," Arya jokes.

Several nurses join our table, and before we know it, time has flown by in fits of laughter.

"Okay, I'll save that story for a rainy day," Arya concedes when a nurse begs her to share another amusing tale.

"Time to get back to work," someone announces.

Arya glances at her watch and gasps. "Shit, I'm in OR with Dr. Torres in ten minutes!" She leaps up, sprinting from the cafeteria.

Suddenly, she skids to a halt and races back. "Your imaginary girlfriend is out of her coma," she pants. "Sorry you didn't get to be the first face she sees. Maybe she would've imprinted on you like a baby duck." She winks before dashing off again.

My heart somersaults — Natalie is awake! I'll finally meet the woman I'm growing obsessed with. What if she's not what I imagined? Or even better, everything I dreamed of and more?

Only one way to find out. The moment of truth has arrived.

With twenty minutes before I'm due back, I race through the halls, nearly colliding with a cranky orderly who mutters some insults my way.

I rush into Natalie's room, pulse thundering. She blinks slowly, still groggy. A grandmotherly nurse smiles and slips out, leaving us alone. I'm breathless as her striking blue eyes meet mine, even more beautiful than I pictured. They hold infinite depth.

"How are you feeling?" My words tumble out, tremulous and unsure.

Natalie frowns, gazing at the bare walls and monitor by her bed.

"Where am I?" she asks.

I swallow, hoping my voice doesn't crack. "You're at Watson Memorial Hospital in Manhattan. You were in a car accident."

She blinks slowly, pinning me with striking blue eyes, processing the information. Though they've likely told her already, it will take time for everything to come back.

"Are you sure this is a hospital?"

"Well, this is not heaven, that's for sure," I joke lamely, hoping for a hint of a smile.

Abruptly, Natalie interrupts my awkward attempts at conversation. "This room is shit. No wonder people get worse in a place like this. I don't want to be here any longer than necessary," she states with a look of disgust.

I stare, stunned into silence. In all my daydreams, she was kind, almost shy. Now, her words sting like a slap.

"Where's my purse?" she demands impatiently.

"I...I don't know. You were in the ICU for a few days. I can ask if you want..."

"Forget it! This gown is hideous," she complains, tugging at the IV line. "Let me take it off."

"Please stop, you'll hurt yourself, and they'll sedate you," I say gently, lightly touching her shoulder. "It has to stay on for now."

I try not to stare as the gown opens, exposing her breasts. At least those exceed my imagination.

"I'll go mad stuck in this place. How long do I have to stay?"

"I'm afraid it will be several days, but I don't oversee your case..."

"Then why are you here?" she interrupts.

"I...I wanted to see how you were. I treated you when you first arrived and helped intubate you," I explain.

Suddenly, her eyes go wide with horror, spotting the bulky cast on her leg. "I'm a dancer. I can't have a broken leg!"

Dr. Patel approaches, amusement flickering across his face. He's been observing us from the doorway for several minutes. "Whether dancer or not, it's definitely broken," he announces, holding up an X-ray. "Those fractured bones are screaming for attention."

At his words, Natalie's face crumples. Fiery anger melts into naked fear.

"Are you in a lot of pain?" I ask gently, wondering if that's the cause of her changed attitude.

"I'm in pain being stuck in this place," she complains with a scowl, glaring around the room.

Dr. Patel chuckles lightly. He sometimes reminds me of the doctor from The Simpsons.

"You think it's funny?" I snap without thinking.

I shouldn't have spoken to him like that, but this situation has me rattled.

"Miss Fey," Dr. Patel interjects, "From this point on, Dr. Harris will be overseeing your care during your hospital stay. I'll speak with Richard about adjusting your schedule," he tells me before exiting, leaving Natalie and me alone.

"Great, now I'm stuck with this useless idiot," Natalie spits, her words like daggers, leaving me speechless.

My pulse thrums as I try to rein in my swirling emotions — confusion, hurt, anger. I want to lash out, to shake her, and demand what happened to the kind, gentle woman of my dreams. But I know that won't help.

Instead, I take a deep breath and perch cautiously on the edge of her bed. "I know you're scared and in pain," I say softly. "But I promise I'll do everything I can to help you get better and back to the stage."

She scoffs and looks away, arms crossed protectively over her chest.

I sigh, wishing I could see beyond this thorny exterior to the real Natalie within or what I hope is the real Natalie. There has to be more to her than biting words.

Chapter 6

Once again, the shrill cry of my alarm clock jolts me awake, and I briefly consider hurling my phone out the window into the dawn light. 5:45 AM. An ungodly hour.

After a rushed shower, I gulp down bitter black coffee, feeling the caffeine bring my sleepy brain back to life. As I arrive at the hospital doors, the rising sun peeks over the horizon, coloring the sky in gorgeous hues. It's so beautiful that for a few seconds, I'm tempted to sit on a bench and watch daybreak unfold.

The cafeteria, my first stop each morning, is nearly empty except for a few nurses and orderlies winding down their night shift, exhaustion etched on their faces. Arya sits at our usual table, her fingers curled around a steaming mug.

"You're early," she remarks as I slide into the seat across from her. "When I was a resident, I was never up this early."

"I want to start the day energized," I reply, sipping my coffee, letting its warmth seep into my bones. "I sleep at night. I'd rather not know what you did as a resident." I tease.

"Oh, those were the days!" Arya sighs wistfully. "How I miss them. Off to see your imaginary girlfriend?"

I nearly choke on my coffee. She still calls Natalie my "imaginary girlfriend." I shouldn't have let my feelings for a patient carry me away. What was I thinking? There's no chance of anything real.

"You know she's not my girlfriend," I mutter.

"Keep telling yourself that, honey. I see the way your eyes light up when you talk about her."

"I just care about her recovery. That's all," I retort unconvincingly.

"Yeah, whatever. By the way, want to know the nurses' nickname for her?"

"I'd rather not, thanks. I'm sure it involves her charming moods."

Arya just smiles knowingly and sips her coffee. I feel my cheeks flush as I picture Natalie's piercing green eyes that seem to see right through me. I know it's hopeless, inappropriate even, but something about her pulls me in like gravity.

With Arya's probing gaze on me, I quickly gulp down the rest of my coffee, trying in vain to push Natalie away from my thoughts.

"Maybe if you go up to her room and hold her hand, whispering sweet nothings in her ear like when she was in a coma, it'll improve her mood," Arya suggests, winking at me.

"I never did that. I just talked to her because it can help coma patients recover," I defend myself, although Arya shakes her head, rolling her eyes.

"You should have gone straight to her room instead of stopping for coffee. You could have caught her naked during her morning bath," she says, glancing at her watch and raising her eyebrows.

I feel my cheeks flush at the thought.

"You're crazy."

"Hey, I got a serious head injury as a kid. Not my fault," she jokes before heading off to work.

When I check the schedule for my morning rounds, I realize Natalie is my very first patient.

"Have fun with that witch," a nurse remarks, pointing at the whiteboard.

"Why do I have her? She's no longer an ER patient. Doesn't she belong to orthopedics now?" I ask.

"We drew straws last night since you weren't here. Sorry, you lost," another resident teases.

"I'm serious, Stephanie," I protest, raising my eyebrows.

"Dr. Patel's orders. You have to coordinate with orthopedics. He left instructions in your locker," she explains.

I shrug resignedly. As residents, we can't protest assignments, even if Dr. Patel is punishing me for yesterday's comment. Little does he know this is no punishment at all for me. Quite the contrary.

"That bitch almost ripped my arm up helping her shower this morning," a nurse complains, showing me her bruised forearm. "Quite the strength for such a petite thing. Must live at the gym."

"She's a dancer," I blurt out without thinking.

"How do you know that?" the nurse asks, puzzled.

"Nothing, I just happen to know. Forget it," I mutter quickly, wanting to escape before I say something improper. It wouldn't look good to admit I spent hours googling and watching videos of a patient online. It's downright creepy, as Arya would say.

Outside Natalie's door, I pause to collect myself before entering.

"Good morning, Natalie," I chime brightly. "How are you feeling today?"

"I'd feel better if I wasn't woken at the crack of dawn. Is there any reason I can't shower at 11 AM? Don't you have water at that time?" she grumbles in response.

"Once you're stronger, you can shower whenever you want. For now, you're still recovering from the accident and need a nurse's help. We need to make sure you don't have any setbacks that could worsen your condition, so we have to work with their schedule," I explain.

I take a deep breath as the image of a naked Natalie in the shower makes me a little nervous. A devilish voice in my head suggests offering to help her shower at noon during my coffee break so she doesn't have to wake early. But I push the unprofessional thought away. Though, for some reason, I can't help picturing her without clothes.

"Can you just leave me alone? I want to sleep," she snaps, turning away from me.

"I'm sorry you're in a bad mood. Let me just check a couple things quickly, and I'll let you rest, okay? In the meantime, can I do anything to help you?"

"You can help by getting out of here and leaving me alone," she retorts bitterly.

I bite my lip. I had imagined our first real interaction so differently. Never thought she'd be this sullen woman before me.

"My back is killing me," Natalie complains with a frown, rubbing her neck. "I barely slept all night. Can I get something other than this rock they call a pillow?"

"Of course. I'll bring a softer one later. Do you need any pain meds or are you managing alright?"

"What I need is for you to fix my leg," she growls.

"My orthopedic colleagues are working on that," I reply with an encouraging smile.

"Today."

"Well, medicine doesn't quite work that way these days. This isn't sci-fi where we zap you in a machine for instant healing. I'd be out of a job," I joke lightly.

But my attempt at humor seems to have the opposite effect based on her scowl.

"Okay, I'll get going. Buzz if you need anything. I'll grab that pillow for you," I say before slipping out the door.

Best not to argue when she's made it clear she's not in the mood for chatter. Each word seems to irritate her more. But I can't help feeling disappointed that the flicker of connection I thought we shared was apparently one-sided.

On the way to the nurses' area, I stop in my tracks and turn around. The visit has been much shorter than I expected, and despite her attitude, I'd like to spend more time with her, so I decide to go get the pillow myself.

It may sound stupid, but I miss our chats in the ICU. More like my monologues, although they helped me tremendously to cope with the demanding workday.

Entering the nearest supply room, I find with relative ease a shelf on which there are several pillows and choose the one that seems the softest of them all. I don't want to get any more complaints from that woman if I can help it.

However, as soon as I am about to leave, the door creaks open, and I find Richard standing in front of me.

"What are you doing here?" I ask nervously when I see he has closed the door behind him.

"I work in this hospital, remember?" My boss answers, sticking closer to me than necessary.

"I'm in a hurry; I'm sorry."

"We're all in a hurry in this hospital, Rachel. I realize you're embarrassed to be seen around your boss, but there's no one here to see us," he whispers, placing a hand on my hip.

"Richard, please. I asked you to keep your distance."

"Don't be silly; I can see how nervous you get when we're alone," he says with a smile that he probably finds seductive, but makes me want to puke.

Instinctively, I place the pillow on my chest and squeeze it as if it were a shield that could protect me.

"I know you feel like it. Your breathing has quickened," he murmurs, stroking my cheek with the back of his hand.

"Richard, get away from me. Please. This is the last time I'm telling you," I threaten, raising my voice a little so he can see I'm serious, even though my whole body is shaking from head to toe.

"Now I'll have to go to the bathroom to think about you," he says, pointing to an obvious erection in his pants.

I wince in disgust and hurry out of there, pressing my hands against the pillow until my knuckles turn white. I know he's not following me, but I can't get the thought out of my head. I can't shake a ridiculous restlessness, as if, for some reason, I'm partly to blame for what's going on.

Shit, I hate that feeling. I have never, at any time, said anything that would make him think I'm interested in anything intimate. It really disgusts me to imagine that he might be stroking his dick in the bathroom while thinking about me right now. I don't know what he's imagining. And yet, I can't seem to shake this stupid feeling of guilt out of my head.

I know I should go to Human Resources and file a complaint. This is going way too far. I don't think he would ever do anything against my will. Still, I don't want to continue with this unpleasant situation. Every time I see Richard, I get too nervous. Coming to work is becoming an ordeal. I didn't go to med school for this.

Maybe there are more young girls in the same situation as me. Other residents or nurses. It's possible that all of us are keeping it a secret out of embarrassment or to keep ourselves out of trouble. All we are doing with our silence makes things more difficult for others.

Once in Natalie's room, I hand her the pillow, but I notice her mood has not improved.

"What took you so long?" she protests.

"I'm sorry."

I soon interrupt myself in the explanation. She turns on the television, ignoring me. And I turn and leave the room in silence.

Disappointment now seems like a heavy slab that has settled right on top of my chest. The contrast between what I had imagined and the reality, a million pitchers of ice water pouring down on my head.

Chapter 7

Arya says it's a violin, but the alarm she's set on my phone to wake me up on night shifts sounds more like a cat being tortured. I have to admit it's the most effective way to wake me up, but it almost gave me a heart attack.

"Alright, alright, I'm up," I grumble, yawning widely and rubbing the sleep from my bleary eyes.

Night shifts are grueling but usually quiet. The frenetic energy of the day giving way to a hushed reverence interrupted only sporadically by the distant beep of monitors or the snores of slumbering patients.

The bright side is that Richard typically sleeps the entire night while on call. My boss makes it abundantly clear he's not to be disturbed unless a patient's life hangs precariously in the balance. So, he gets paid to catch up on beauty rest while the residents do all the actual work.

After giving myself a good full-body stretch, I grab an icy cold energy drink from the fridge to help rouse my groggy mind and body. The frosty aluminum can feels refreshing against my palms as I swiftly crack it open and guzzle down the contents in several deep gulps. The caffeine has yet to kick in, and my brain is still muddled and lethargic.

My shoes make no sound as I pad down the worn linoleum floors on my way to check the assignment whiteboard. There are a few new admissions overnight, but I'm mostly tasked with routine overnight checks on our regular patients to ensure all remain stable.

The assignment board awaits. There are the usual scribbles - fresh admissions, notes, and updates. But it's the familiar names I'm after, those whose stories I know by heart.

Even after she awoke from her coma, a very different woman than the imagined angel I'd foolishly conjured, some naive part of me still clings to those fanciful daydreams. A small, unreasonable pocket of hope still yearns for her to somehow be the woman of my dreams.

I take her medical records and walk briskly down the hallway. In front of her door, I pause to take a deep breath and calm myself before quietly stepping into the room.

She looks so peaceful in her sleep. Her relaxed, steady, rhythmic breathing takes me back to those days when I visited her in the intensive care unit. To those short visits when I would sit next to her and tell her what was going on in my life or the naïve plans my head was making for when we would be together.

Today, I look back and am almost ashamed to admit it, but it was so real to me that it scared me. I imagined her eyes lighting up when she saw me for the first time or maybe laughing together at a romantic dinner, exchanging kisses and pretty words, holding hands on the tablecloth.

"Get it together, Rachel."

I shake my head slightly to banish my old daydreams and carefully check her vitals. Her skin is as smooth as silk and transmits a wonderful warmth. The fact that her nipples are marked through the thin fabric of the hospital gown does not help my concentration at all.

After checking and rechecking that all her vitals are normal, I dim the lights again and get ready to leave the room when a figure startles me.

"Well, well, my favorite resident," my boss whispers.

"Richard, what are you doing here? There's no emergency," I say nervously.

I'm starting to get too tired of this situation.

"What do you say we have breakfast together at the Starbucks across the street when the shift is over?" he proposes.

"When my shift is over, I'll go to sleep," I assure him dryly.

"Alone?"

"Alone."

"Wouldn't it be better to do it with someone else?" He keeps his voice very low, but his cockiness makes me want to spit in his face.

"Do you need something, Richard?"

"You know what I need from you," he replies. "And you also know that I always get what I want one way or another," he adds, sticking too close to me.

"I told you I'm not interested. Not now, not ever," I snap, but he doesn't seem to be giving up.

"Do I have to go to the bathroom to think about you again?"

I take a deep breath, trying to stay calm, but just then, Natalie turns around and looks uneasy. No doubt we have inadvertently raised our voices and disturbed her sleep.

And fortunately for me, Richard becomes flustered, leaving the room without even looking back.

"What time is it?" Natalie sighs.

"Almost three in the morning. I just wanted to check on you and make sure your vitals are okay. I'm sorry I woke you," I apologize.

Natalie nods and yawns. Then, to my surprise, I hear a vague "thank you" in a very low tone of voice that makes my legs shake.

And as soon as I return home from the night shift, I can't stop thinking about her despite the fatigue building up in my body.

She was so beautiful, so calm. Now that the bruises are almost healed, her face is beautiful. And...fuck, the fabric of the gowns we put on the patients is too thin...those nipples refuse to leave my mind.

Before realizing what I'm doing, I slip my right hand under my pajama pants and feel the arousal between my legs. I sigh and run my fingertips over my belly, moving up to brush against the underside of my breasts. I imagine it's Natalie doing it, and I feel her soft touch on every inch of my skin.

Slight moans escape me as I feel my thumb hardening my nipples, though, in my mind, it is Natalie's tongue caressing them, muffling wonderful gasps in them.

My breathing quickens, and I squeeze my thighs together in anticipation as I stroke my pubis. Unable to wait any longer, I undo my pajama pants, kicking them away from the bed.

I feel shivers as I imagine Natalie sliding her fingers through the wetness of my sex, stroking me slowly as she smiles at me, making me moan with pleasure as soon as she slips two fingers inside me.

I begin to touch myself at a steady pace. Between moans, I alternate it with light caresses on my clit, imagining my whole body trembling under her hands, arching my back in pleasure, and almost feeling Natalie's palm rubbing my clit as she fingers me.

"Fuck," I cry out as I feel her bringing me to the brink of orgasm without knowing it.

I get up from the bed with my breath hitching and rummage through the dresser drawer where I keep my toys. I grab a bottle of my favorite lubricant and awkwardly pour it over my fingers.

I got into the habit of using it with a former partner, and since then, I love the feeling of my fingers sliding across my sex.

Almost without realizing it, I close my eyes. Again, Natalie appears in my imagination. She gently spreads the lube between my legs, stopping first at the entrance to my sex, pressing it before moving up towards my clit. Reaching it, she makes some circles around it, avoiding it, simply letting some of the lube spread over that area before making a "V" with her fingers and placing my lips between them.

I lift my hips, feeling the pleasure of her fingers sliding between my lips, getting closer and closer to my clit each time. Natalie smiles at me. She gazes at me, as if to check how much pleasure she is giving me.

Between moans, my breath coming in gasps, I beg her to come closer to it, to press it, but she only smiles.

With a seductive wink, she makes a "V" with her fingers again, though instead of my lips, she traps my clit between them, initiating a rhythmic movement that makes me tremble with desire.

"I need it now, please," I sigh, unable to hold on any longer.

Natalie gives me a beautiful smile and slips her middle finger between my lips, pressing against the entrance of my sex without actually entering.

She does this several times, each time pressing a bit harder. Every now and then, she inserts her finger a little inside me, only to withdraw it and leave me with a feeling of emptiness that is impossible to bear.

"Natalie," I hiss, rooting my fingers in her mane as I gasp into her ear.

Finally, she heeds my pleas, and two of her fingers slip inside me. She keeps up a steady rhythm, the splashing in and out of my sex the only sound in the bedroom, broken only by my moans. In my excitement, I don't even realize that Natalie's gasps are only in my mind.

I repeat her name over and over, as if that might increase the intensity. I tense my back, my legs tremble, and Natalie gives me one of the best orgasms I can remember.

I drop to the mattress, fingers still inside me, as little spasms of pleasure follow one after another. Only when I open my eyes, it's not Natalie's, but mine that are still inside me.

And, as I catch my breath, sleep takes over my body. Naked in bed, I think of Natalie, of her small nipples poking through the robe's fabric. Her smile. Of that whispered "thank you" in her sleep. I think of the incredible orgasm she's unknowingly gifted me with.

Shit. This is getting too serious.

Chapter 8

The hospital halls seem even busier than usual this morning. I offer quick smiles and greetings to the gaggle of nurses whispering amongst themselves as I make my way briskly to room 305.

Though visiting Natalie once filled me with a sense of joy and purpose, now it mostly causes growing feelings of concern and anxiety churning in the pit of my stomach. Her bitter attitude and callous selfishness pain me too much.

Of course, I understand how shocking it must be to wake from a coma and be told you were in a serious car accident. And having your leg shattered must be utterly devastating news for a professional dancer in the prime of her career.

Were I in her shoes, I'd surely be outraged at the injustice of it all, too. But the hospital staff are here solely to help her recuperate, not to bear the brunt of misdirected frustration. Perhaps I simply idealized her true nature.

Upon entering the room, I see Natalie sitting up in bed reading a novel, seeming uncharacteristically relaxed for once. The monitor beside her beeps and hums rhythmically, the blinking numbers conveying her steady vital signs in the esoteric language of medicine. And there she is — the woman who's filled my thoughts near-constantly for days on end now. My imaginary girlfriend returned to the land of the living, as Arya jokingly puts it.

Natalie glances up from her book briefly as I enter, our eyes meeting for a lingering moment. To my immense surprise, her lips turn up into a faint but unmistakable smile — the very first I've seen cross her face since she awoke.

"Good morning, Natalie. How did you manage to sleep last night?" I ask politely, going about checking her vital signs as usual.

"Oh, just living the high life here in this luxury suite, with its many fine distractions," she replies sarcastically, a wry twinkle in her eye.

I raise my eyebrows in momentary surprise at her unexpectedly lighthearted quip. She seems to be in a rare good mood today. No shouting or hurling unreasonable demands just yet. No blaming me for anything and everything wrong with her world. Could it be we're making actual progress here? I don't dare get my hopes up just yet.

She remains silent as I wrap the blood pressure cuff around her arm and pump it tight. However, it seems a more comfortable, companionable silence than tense or hostile.

"So, what's the deal with the creeper doctor who was lurking around here last night?" she asks suddenly, eyeing me closely as I slide the thermometer under her tongue.

I freeze up momentarily. "I'm not sure who you mean," I deflect weakly, my voice clearly faltering. I can feel my cheeks start to burn crimson, avoiding her gaze.

"Oh, don't play dumb with me. That guy was clearly a total pig," she retorts bluntly, lip curled in disgust.

"You...heard all that?" I ask faintly, mortified.

"Kind of hard to sleep with some pig pawing all over my doctor just a few feet away," Natalie replies sarcastically, one eyebrow raised.

Thorough humiliation washes over me in waves as I stand there tongue-tied. I wish the floor would just open up and swallow me whole right about now. This is beyond embarrassing.

"I'm sorry, you shouldn't have had to hear it. It happens, you know. It's no big deal, it's nothing serious," I mumble, although the humiliation I feel runs through every atom of my body.

"No big deal? It didn't seem like no big deal to me. And those things shouldn't happen. In fact, I had to make noise to make him stop because he was already rubbing his dick on your ass, if I remember correctly. That's no joke, Dr. Harris, it's a very serious matter," she insists, staring at me.

"I'd rather stop this conversation. It's not what you're imagining, and I have to keep checking your vitals because I have more patients to see."

It pains me to respond like this. She's worrying about me right now, but I hardly know her at all. It's one thing to get my hopes up while Natalie was in a coma. Even to touch myself thinking about her last night. It's quite another to trust this woman with such a sensitive subject and one that could cause me too much trouble.

I know I should put a stop to this situation. I am the first one interested in doing so, but I must evaluate the steps to follow very well. Richard is too powerful an enemy.

"Look, for what it's worth, I know exactly what you're going through. In fact, I had to go through a similar thing when I was only sixteen years old, and it was very hard," she interrupts suddenly.

"Sixteen?" I ask, raising my eyebrows in surprise.

"It was my first chance to get a professional contract as a dancer, and the producer was very unethical. He insisted on being present while I was changing my clothes. He took the opportunity to grope me in the dressing room. I remember feeling horrible. I cried for days. I just wanted to dance, not to go through such a situation. I trembled every time I saw him. I swear those were the worst days of my life," Natalie confesses, biting her lower lip in a wince.

"I don't know if I want to hear how it goes on," I say fearfully.

"Luckily for me, I was saved by the most unlikely person. The woman who hated me the most in that company was a dancer on the decline. She knew that her days on stage were over, and I would be the one to replace her in the future. She made my life impossible from the first day I arrived. Instead, she once saw me crying after talking to the show's producer. She hugged me and, without saying anything to me, assured me that she would not let him come any closer. From that day on, she would stick to me to prevent me from being alone with that pig."

"It must have been really tough," I admit.

"You can't imagine. If you're having a hard time now, imagine what it's like when you're sixteen. But I learned from the experience, and I didn't let it happen again. My dignity is above my job; normally, they back down and stop. Still, there's always a pig like that doctor out there. Luckily, in my job, underage girls are never left alone now," she explains.

"Richard is my boss, and he has excellent contacts, so I guess it's complicated," I confess with a long sigh as I sit next to her on the edge of the bed. "Still, I can't believe he won't take no for an answer when he's married. I refuse every time, but..."

"He doesn't get the hint," Natalie finishes the sentence for me.

"Yeah, basically, he's not getting the hint. I wish I didn't have to see him every day at work. It's becoming very uncomfortable and very unprofessional. Luckily, in a few months, I'll choose a specialty, and I'll be able to run away from him," I explain.

Natalie takes my hand in hers and tilts her head to one side before continuing to speak.

"Did you tell anyone else?"

"It would just be my word against his. Richard is the head of the Emergency Department, and his father-in-law is on the Board of Directors of this hospital. I'm sure he'd find a way to retaliate if a formal complaint was filed," I admit with a shrug.

"It's possible. Be careful, okay?" Sometimes, guys like that don't know when to stop.

"Thank you," I whisper.

"Besides, something tells me that even if he weren't married or if he was younger, your preferences don't go in that direction," she says as I'm about to leave.

I'm stunned. Not knowing what to say.

"What?"

"Am I wrong?" Natalie asks with a charming smile. "I don't think so. I've seen the way you look at my nipples," she adds with a wink.

"I'm sorry. I never meant to stare and...."

"What makes you think it bothers me?"

I take a deep breath in an attempt to calm down because, at this moment, I don't even know where to hide. My hands are sweating, and I've become so nervous I think my whole body is shaking.

"I've been told that you were very concerned about me when I was in a coma in the ICU," she says, changing the subject of conversation, probably when she notices that I'm about to have a heart attack. "Thank you very much, I really appreciate it."

"It's been a pleasure. I was one of the first people who took care of you when you arrived at the hospital, and I was very impressed to see you like that," I assure her.

"Be careful with that pig, okay?" Natalie says goodbye, and I swear the smile she gives me sends me floating down the corridors until my next visit.

Chapter 9

The jarring shriek of my alarm clock viciously drags me from a deep slumber, and I'm sorely tempted to grab the offensive device and hurl it forcefully across the room.

Why, in God's name, did I choose this grueling profession again? The positively brutal hours will marginally improve once I finally attain an attending physician position. Still, medicine is eternally demanding, requiring constant sacrifice.

With a mighty effort, I drag myself from the warm embrace of my bed to stumble bleary-eyed to the bathroom. The harsh fluorescent lighting of the mirror reflects back an exhausted, drained woman with dark undereye circles that no amount of makeup could possibly cure. With a resigned sigh, I step into the shower, letting the strong cascade of hot water revive my weary body and mind, thousands of water droplets massaging away the last stubborn cobwebs of fatigue.

After thoroughly drying off and applying just enough makeup to adequately mask the obvious tiredness, I zombie-walk my way to the kitchen to guzzle a strong coffee before embarking on the drive to the hospital. Just another day trying to heal, comfort, and hopefully make some small positive difference in my patients' lives.

The dazzling golden light of dawn spills brilliantly over New York's concrete jungle as I drive, glinting brightly off the huge glass expanses of the looming skyscrapers surrounding me.

Nicole, my old roommate, constantly chided me for driving to work when we had a subway station right outside the front door of my apartment building. But despite the chaos and frustrations of big city traffic, driving somehow relaxes me. I've grown so accustomed to the daily grind of traffic jams and bike couriers madly darting about that I barely even notice anymore.

At the second stoplight, I quickly text Arya while the car idles:

Rachel: Almost there. Coffee's on me this morning!

Her rapid reply flashes on my phone barely a minute later.

Arya: You're an angel fallen straight from heaven! Meet at Starbucks, please, not the crap hospital cafeteria. I'll order for us both, don't worry!

Rachel: It's a date! ;)

I can't help but smile to myself, feeling my mood lift. Arya never fails to brighten my day, no matter how bone-tired I may be. It's like her bubbly energy transfers by sheer osmosis.

After parking in the cramped hospital lot, I immediately spot Arya enthusiastically waving at me from our usual corner table tucked away inside Starbucks. Her hair is already mussed and coming loose from her ponytail despite not having officially started our shift yet. She always jokes this is absolutely the perfect table for people watching and spying on other customers — claims in her next life she'll be CIA, no question.

"How's my favorite resident doing on this spectacular Monday morning?" Arya asks brightly, eagerly pushing my large steaming coffee and a tasty-looking muffin across the table toward me.

"You sure know how to make a woman melt, offering me a coffee and a muffin," I joke. "How was your weekend?"

"The usual chaos. On Saturday, Nicole and Inés came over for dinner with their daughter, who dyed Patricia's dog blue. Before that, she chewed on a pen until it discharged in her mouth and left blue handprints all over the poor dog's fur," she explains, rolling her eyes.

"Your goddaughter's going to be a handful. She learns fast."

"She has poor Inés in despair. We'll keep the baby next weekend so she and Nicole can rest and have a couple's life. The girl insists on sleeping with them and, as they are half stupid, they leave her. They are spoiling that kid," Arya protests, shaking her head.

"It seems to me that her godmother is the first one to spoil her."

"But that's my job as godmother. I have to spoil her. Her mothers are the ones who have to raise and educate her," Arya jokes with a shrug. "How are things going with your imaginary girlfriend?"

"She's recovering nicely from her injuries."

"Yeah, yeah, her health is fine. And between you two, is she still the same asshole? Because what a girlfriend you've chosen," she adds with a dramatic gesture as she brings a hand to her forehead.

"You're such a pain in the ass! But things have improved a lot. Yesterday, we had a conversation that really surprised me," I admit, and a silly smile appears on my lips.

"Oh, what a love-struck face you make when you talk about the dancer!"

"You're such an asshole!"

"Wow, here comes your favorite doctor," Arya announces, pointing with her chin towards the door, where Richard's huge figure appears.

"Shit! Oh, fuck. I can't even have a quiet coffee," I complain, letting out a long sigh.

"Ignore him, he's a fucking asshole."

"And my boss."

"A fucking asshole of a boss, then," Arya says with a smile.

"Yeah, that's easier said than done," I protest.

And if I don't feel comfortable around him, Richard keeps trying. He approaches our table after ordering a coffee, shuffling his feet as if some supernatural being had stolen all his energy.

"Can I sit with you two?" he asks with a smile.

"Seats are taken," Arya blurts out without even having to think about it.

My boss looks at her in confusion. He then looks at the two empty chairs at our table and looks back at Arya as if wondering if she is joking or serious.

"Fu, fu, Richard. There are a lot of empty tables in that part of the café," Arya points to the other end of the room.

The poor man doesn't seem to understand anything. Still, he shrugs his shoulders and walks reluctantly to one of the tables Arya has pointed out.

"He's going to make me pay for this," I whisper, leaning toward her.

"Fuck him. He's a dick."

***

The sharp antiseptic smell hits me as soon as I enter the hospital, both repelling and comforting me. It's the ever-present reminder that life and death walk hand in hand within these walls.

"Good morning again, sunshine," Richard greets me, a slimy grin on his face as he follows Arya and me inside after our coffee.

I resist the urge to roll my eyes. This man grows more inappropriate by the day. Sunshine? Really?

"I'm still waiting for an answer about dinner," he says, sidling up to me when no one's looking. "Remember, I'm evaluating residents next week."

"I'm quite busy with rounds, Richard," I reply dismissively, gathering patient charts.

"You might want to think it over. Evaluations next week," he reminds pointedly before sauntering off down the hall.

I let out an exasperated sigh. With all the real daily problems and family dramas, he's focused on bedding a resident twenty years his junior. This man is so disgusting.

My heart clenches as I enter little Kai's room. The three-year-old battles leukemia bravely while her mother watches on, eyes brimming with worry and fatigue. I wish I could embrace her, absorb some of her pain.

Arya visits Kai often, bringing toys and stories, a beacon of hope who conquered the same illness as a child. Seeing them together fills me with light. The kid adores her almost as much as I do.

After rounding, it's time to see Natalie. Evaluations today will determine her treatment plan and possible discharge. I'm thrilled about her recovery but know I'll miss our visits, as prickly as she can be.

She intrigues me, challenges me.

With her, I feel alive.

Chapter 10

Today holds the weight of a thousand expectations for Natalie. As I enter her hospital room, flanked by Richard, a pair of nurses, and a neurologist, I silently pray that the CT scan hasn't revealed any brain damage.

I know the fury simmering beneath her skin, the broken leg a cruel taunt to her dancer's spirit. Yet, given the accident, it's a miracle she's even breathing. A snapped bone, even for a ballerina, is a hurdle, not a dead end. And once she's healed, with the right rehab, dancing could be a possibility. Above all, her life will roll on, unhindered.

Her skin, pale as moonlight, seems to shimmer under the harsh fluorescent glow. Even in that horrendous pale blue hospital gown, she is breathtaking. As she catches sight of me, a subtle smile flickers across her face, quickly replaced by a scowl as she notices Richard's presence.

"Alright, let's get started," Richard announces without any semblance of a greeting. His voice, deep as a canyon, reverberates in the constricted space. "Follow my finger with your eyes," he commands.

My boss lifts his index finger, moving it across her field of vision, but Natalie's sapphire eyes remain unmoving. Static. A grunt from Richard shatters the strained silence.

He repeats the instruction, this time slower, but the result is just the same. Natalie remains still as a statue, her eyes twin pools of icy blue, and for a fleeting moment, my heart stalls. I conjure up a myriad of dire scenarios, which I quickly dispel, concluding that she's merely refusing to comply with Richard.

With a huff, Richard proceeds with a series of basic neurological tests, commanding Natalie to perform simple tasks.

"Push against my hands. Touch your nose with your fingertip. Recite the months of the year backward," he barks one command after another, but she continues to ignore them. Richard scans the CT results in search of some damage, his brows furrowing in confusion.

I bite the inside of my cheek to suppress a grin. My boss is chasing after an injury that simply doesn't exist. Natalie's defiance might be almost childish, but I'd be lying if I said I didn't relish seeing Richard so rattled. His usual swagger and bravado have vanished.

"Can you cooperate?" he grits out, his words rushed.

"Can you ask nicely?" Natalie retorts, inspecting her nails with an air of nonchalance.

Richard's neck flushes, reminiscent of a cartoon character on the verge of exploding. He inhales sharply, searching for the right words. The nurses exchange glances, and the room fills with tension, like the heavy air before a storm. Accustomed to control, losing it leaves him scrambling.

"Natalie, could you please follow my finger?" His words are polite, but his tone seethes with restrained irritation.

"Since you've finally remembered your manners, I don't see why not," she replies, her stunning eyes smoothly following Richard's finger.

With each test, my boss grows increasingly agitated, his breathing more rapid and ragged. Natalie only complies when asked politely and seems to delight in pushing him to his limits. She even winks at me when Richard's back is turned.

By the time we reach the reflex test, Richard is fit to burst. His jaw clenched tight, a thin sheen of sweat glistening on his forehead.

Without warning, he strikes Natalie's healthy knee with the small hammer, but she doesn't flinch.

"Let me try," I suggest, my voice timid and unsure.

I take the tool from Richard, feeling the warm metal in my palm.

"Natalie, I'm going to test your reflexes, okay? You'll barely feel it," I assure her with a gentle smile, and she nods.

I tap lightly under her kneecap with precision, and her leg twitches slightly.

"Perfect. The reflexes are just fine," I confirm, shifting my gaze to the nurses to avoid the blistering glare of my boss.

The two nurses let loose a soft, nervous titter, a sound that seems to be the final straw for Richard. Before I can react, he seizes my arm, his grip unnecessarily tight, hauling me into the hallway. His thick fingers dig painfully into my bicep, and I'm half afraid I'll wear their marks come morning.

"What the hell was that?" he demands, his voice low and laced with barely suppressed anger. His breath, a mix of stale coffee and lingering smoke, makes me turn my face slightly away.

I shrug, rubbing my aching arm, choosing silence over words that might stoke his ire further.

"What's with that woman? I won't stand for such disrespect in front of my staff," he declares as if the apparent loss of authority is all he cares about.

"She seems to respond better when asked politely," I suggest, carefully choosing my words. "It's not that hard," I add.

"Oh, please, she's a diva. Acts like a spoiled five-year-old. Maybe she's used to being the center of attention on Broadway, but here, she's a nobody," he retorts.

And therein lies the crux of the issue. To Richard, patients are nobodies. They don't matter, they're just numbers: Room 105, Room 314. At some point in his mind, they've lost every shred of humanity and have become nothing but data.

I've never seen him this riled up. His face is tinged with an unsettling shade of crimson. It's as if his anger is simmering, on the verge of boiling over any moment.

Just then, the two nurses exit the room, bidding Natalie a pleasant goodbye, and pass by us.

"Are you done with the reports?" my boss asks, his expression stormy.

One of the nurses, a robust woman with deep-set eyes, nods. A small, satisfied smile plays on her lips.

They clutch the medical charts against their chests and head towards the nursing station. For a moment, it seems Richard wants to leave too, but suddenly, he halts, pivots on his heels, and storms back into Natalie's room, his fists clenched tight.

I fear what might happen next, so I linger by the door, prepared to step in if needed, though I sincerely hope it doesn't come to that.

"You seem to get along well with my staff when I'm not around," he accuses, his tone venomous. "What's your issue with me, huh?"

Richard raises his voice, attempting to intimidate her, asserting his towering presence beside her bed. But Natalie looks at him with a nearly amused expression.

"Maybe I don't like men who harass women," she retorts calmly.

And while my heart might've missed a beat, I think Richard's might need a crash cart any second now.

"What did you say?" he demands, his face shifting from a fiery red to a dangerous shade of purple.

The tension in the room is palpable, a live wire ready to spark. But beneath it all, there's an undeniable undercurrent of something more — a subtle dance of power, a delicate balance of respect, a hint of a brewing storm.

"Last night, I heard you. I saw you with my own eyes, trying to take advantage of Dr. Harris," Natalie's words cut through the silence like a knife. "Even when she said no, over and over, you didn't stop. I don't know where it would have ended if I hadn't made a noise. You were grinding against her like a damn pig."

"I don't know what you think you saw or heard, but..."

"Exactly what I just told you," Natalie's voice is like ice, calm and unyielding. "And I won't hesitate to confirm it to hospital management, Human Resources, or whoever else takes care of those things around here."

"I didn't... it wasn't exactly like that..." Richard stammers, his voice trembling.

"You better start treating women with more dignity and respect. We're not pieces of meat. You're old enough to have your hormones under control," Natalie admonishes.

Her words ring with authority, making Richard cower.

"Now that you know why I won't cooperate with you, and why I do with the rest of the staff, get out of my room," she commands, her chin juts toward the door.

Richard stands there, mouth agape, in the deafening silence that follows. Then, with a slump of his shoulders, he leaves the room, not even noticing me standing by the door.

I'm left in a state of shock, watching Richard's once imposing figure shrink as he retreats down the hallway.

In the room, Natalie turns on the TV, laughing at an old '90s sitcom.

"That was... that was incredible," I admit, my eyebrows raised in awe.

She smiles, turns off the TV, and pats the bed, inviting me to sit. Her blue eyes are kind, almost unrecognizable.

"Thank you," I sigh. "I should've reported him, but I can't muster the courage."

Natalie covers my hand with hers, her skin impossibly soft.

"It's not always easy when they hold power over you. And from what you've told me, he's well-connected. Even in normal cases, no one wants to relive that kind of experience. Somehow, women always end up on the losing side, forced to prove we're victims."

"I know. I've thought about it too many times," I confess, letting out a heavy sigh.

Natalie squeezes my hand and smiles, one of those smiles that make you forget all your troubles. And for some reason, I can faintly smell the fragrant aroma of her shampoo.

"You're not alone in this," she says, her voice musical yet strong. "If and when you're ready, I'll be right by your side. We'll do this together."

My eyes start to glisten as I'm overcome with gratitude.

"Together," I echo in a whisper.

Chapter 11

I hesitate in the doorway, my fingers clenched tight around the fresh flower bouquet. Its sweet aroma does little to calm the storm of emotions swelling within me.

Here I stand, grappling with feelings I shouldn't harbor for one of my patients. Whispers of temptation, far too sweet, far too alluring.

I take a deep breath, remind myself of professional boundaries, and step inside. Without a word, I set the flowers on the bedside table.

"What's this?" Natalie's voice cuts through the silence, tinged with amusement.

I smile softly at the bouquet, now looking out of place against the sterile white surface. "I thought you might like some flowers to brighten up the room." My explanation sounds feeble, even to my own ears.

"I'm allergic."

"Oh God, I'm so sorry! I'll take them right out. I wasn't thinking," I rush to apologize.

"Kidding, just kidding. Hey, come back!" Natalie laughs. "You should see your face."

I exhale sharply. "Don't joke about allergies in a hospital."

"Lighten up, Rachel," she chuckles, then winces. "Don't make me laugh; everything still hurts from the car accident."

I shake my head, unable to keep from smiling. Her laughter is musical, contagious — the kind you want to keep hearing.

"So, if it wasn't just for decoration, why the flowers?" She raises a brow, biting her lip in a way that makes my pulse quicken.

"Gratitude, I suppose," I reply, though the word hangs limply between us.

"For the thing with Dr. Grabby Hands?"

I nod, swallowing hard as I grasp for the right words. "You stood up for me when I felt powerless. Showed strength when I had none." My voice wavers slightly.

Natalie just smiles softly as we let the muffled sounds of the hospital fill the silence — distant beeps, hushed voices, the subtle stench of antiseptic.

"It was nothing," she finally says, shifting over to make room beside her.

I sit, our shoulders lightly touching. "It meant everything to me. You barely knew me, but spoke with such conviction. No one has ever..." I trail off, losing my nerve.

Natalie tilts her head, looking at me intently. "Yet you sat with me for hours in the ICU. The nurses told me so." She pauses, then grins. "Probably crossing some professional line there, doctor."

I begin to protest, but Natalie places a slender finger to my lips. "I'm teasing. It was incredibly thoughtful of you." Her touch is electric, warming my entire body. She leaves her hand there a beat too long, and I wonder if she can feel the frantic thrumming of my heart.

Natalie's radiant smile suddenly fades, her azure eyes clouding with worry. "Do you think I'll ever dance again? No one will give me a straight answer."

I sigh heavily, lowering my voice. "I don't know, Natalie. I wish I could tell you for sure."

Natalie nods, her slender throat bobbing as she swallows.

"A full recovery is possible, that's for sure, but returning to professional dance depends on how you heal. It's an incredibly demanding career, and your injuries were severe."

Natalie closes her eyes, long lashes fanning across her pale cheeks.

I continue gently, "Our physiotherapy department is one of the best in the country. They'll help you through rehabilitation." I shrug helplessly. "But right now, it's just too soon to know if you'll dance again. I'm sorry I don't have a better answer."

"Thank you for being honest," Natalie whispers, grasping my hand tightly between both of hers. "Dance is my lifeblood. I don't know what I'd do if..." Her voice catches, and she takes a shuddering breath. "It's my art, my self-expression. The thought of losing it terrifies me."

A comfortable silence settles between us, the walls receding until it feels like we're encapsulated in our own intimate world. The soft hum of the AC becomes a lullaby.

"You know, I hated you at first," Natalie admits suddenly.

I blink in surprise. "You hated me? Why?"

"With your perfect smile, so eager to help. Little Miss Perfect. And I was just so angry at myself for the accident." She pauses, looking away. "I jeopardized everything by driving recklessly. I'm such an idiot."

I wait quietly for her to continue.

"But then I realized you care because you're genuinely a good person, not just doing your job or people-pleasing." She meets my eyes again. "When they told me how you worried over me in the coma...it was sweet. That and, well, you are incredibly hot."

"W-what?" I stammer, blushing furiously.

"Rachel, look at me," Natalie says firmly, squeezing my hand. "We both feel there's something more here. Don't play dumb, we're both adults."

My heart hammers wildly as the air grows heavy with unspoken words. Natalie trails her fingers up my arm, leaving a trail of fire in their wake. Our eyes lock, gazes colliding like planets pulled into each other's orbit. My body sways unconsciously toward hers, muscles taut with anticipation.

And it's Natalie who breaks the silence, her voice soft and hesitant.

"You know, I've always put up walls around myself. All my life. Ever since I got my first professional contract at sixteen, I've tried to keep people at a distance. Maybe it's easier that way," she confesses.

"It's a defense mechanism. We all have it in one way or another," I nod in response.

"And yet here you are, breaking through those strong walls without even trying."

I get lost in the depths of her blue eyes, in her beautiful smile, and the world fades away. In her gaze, there is a raw intensity. At once, a primal desire and a vulnerability I've never seen before. It is intoxicating and terrifying at the same time.

"Why did you care so much about me?" Natalie asks, sitting up with difficulty to be closer.

"Because you're worth it," I answer, trying to find the right words amidst a whirlwind of emotions.

Suddenly, the distance that separates us seems enormous and minuscule at the same time. Every glance is loaded with meaning, with deep feelings that dance around us.

"Come here," she sighs, pulling my arm towards her.

For a few moments, time stands still. Our lips are just inches apart, and I feel a strange tightness in my chest that makes my breathing quicken. Every fiber of my skin screams for me to close the gap between us, to lose myself in the moment.

I close my eyes for an instant, almost floating on a cloud, and when her lips brush mine, it feels like the most wonderful thing I've ever felt. They caress me slowly, half-open, the tip of her tongue seeking to slip between my lips without me being able to kiss her back.

"I'm so sorry, Natalie," I apologize, looking away.

"What's wrong with you?"

Suddenly, I am speechless. An abyss full of desire and regret. My mind is a hornet's nest of ideas, torn between the pull of my heart and common sense. Everything seems to go by too fast. Thoughts fly without me being able to catch any of them. My profession, ethics, responsibility, hospital rules?

"Are you going to tell me what's wrong with you?" Natalie insists.

"You are my patient."

"I'm a grown woman, and right now, you want me as much as I want you. Don't try to deny it."

"I'm not denying it," I admit.

"Then why did you stop? It's just a kiss, damn it. It's just a fucking kiss."

"What do you want?" I ask fearfully.

"I think what I want is pretty clear, but if you'd rather I put it into words, it's no problem. Right now, what I want... No... what I need is for you to slip a hand under the sheet and fuck me until I cum," she breathes, her breath coming in ragged gasps.

"Shit!"

Instinctively, I look down at her nipples, peeking hard through the thin fabric of the robe, and my mind clouds over.

"Natalie, I have feelings for you. I don't mean to deny it," I confess as I pull away slightly, trying to create both physical and emotional distance. "I'd like to get to know you more, but it's complicated. You're my patient, and there are lines we can't cross."

"I want to get to know you more, too, but right now, I need a different kind of attention. Like having an orgasm, for example. We'll have time to get to know each other later," she explains in rapid-fire words.

"It's not that simple."

"It seems so to me. There's no one else here. The door is closed; the way you have me, it will go very fast. Just slip your hand under the sheets and keep going..." she insists.

"I think I'd better go," I announce, and as soon as I get up, I feel our distance widening, not only in physical space but also in emotional space. A moment ago, full of intimacy, the room now feels a strange feeling of guilt and disappointment.

"Rachel, wait. I'm sorry I was too direct. Stay a little longer, please," she asks, stretching out her hand to me.

"If things were different, maybe..."

"I wish they were," she interrupts, and her eyes have turned sad.

***

"Wait, wait. Explain it to me all over again, I don't get it," Arya repeats, opening her huge eyes wide.

"What the hell don't you get, Arya?"

"Did she really ask you to fuck her? Just like that? Shit, why don't things like that happen to me?"

"Just like that. And keep your voice down. You know how rumors spread in this hospital," I protest.

"I hate to tell you about it, but the rumor train between you and your imaginary girlfriend has long since departed. Since the days when you spent your romantic evenings with her in the ICU, more or less," Arya explains with a shrug.

"Fuck this place," I complain, clicking my tongue.

"Now, what's the problem? You've been imagining sexual fantasies about that dancer for weeks, ever since she was in a coma, and you didn't know if she would recover. I'm not even asking you what kind of fantasies you've been having..."

"Arya, for fuck's sake! Stop it."

"I said I'm not going to ask you. I'm sure they're very kinky. But seriously, it's your dream come true, right?" She asks, opening her hands.

"No, it isn't."

"How so? What do you mean, no?"

"Remind you that it's forbidden? Natalie is my patient, in case you've forgotten. Not even a patient at the hospital. She's my patient," I punctuate, separating each syllable as if I'm trying to force it into her mind.

"What's she got until she's discharged, a week? Two at the most?"

"Surely one," I confirm.

"Well, you're in big trouble then, aren't you? The wait will be endless," Arya jokes, "Did I tell you that Liam, my wife's son, was my patient?"

"I'd rather not know about that story, really," I hasten to answer, covering my ears.

"It was nothing illegal, you dumbass," Arya protests. "What I'm trying to tell you is that we were fooling around without doing anything, and then, as soon as Liam stopped being my patient, we started dating. Nothing is stopping you from doing that."

"I don't know."

"What's bothering you? You don't seem convinced," she insists, raising her eyebrows.

"Maybe I'm a little traditional, but I didn't like her reaction today," I explain, letting out a little huff. "Guess she was… too direct for my taste."

"You do the opposite, then," Arya suggests. "Prepare some nice gesture for her. Let her see that you're a hopeless romantic, one of those that don't exist anymore, and that you want a real relationship and not just sex. If she doesn't want the same, tough luck. Hey, and if all she needs is an urgent favor, just a quicky, let me know. All I want is for the girl to recover as soon as possible," Arya jokes with a wink of the eye.

Chapter 12

The memory of our electrifying kiss lingers as I hesitantly approach Natalie's hospital room, tension hanging thick in the air. She sits rigidly upright in bed, backlit by the hazy morning light filtering through the curtains. The soft glow lends an ethereal luminescence to her soft skin, and I'm momentarily transfixed.

Natalie's delicate jaw is tightly clenched, her brow furrowed in frustration as she argues with the physical therapist.

"For the tenth time, I cannot do that movement," she insists, an edge of brittle impatience in her usually musical voice.

The therapist, an athletic woman likely in her mid-forties, glances up with sympathy rather than annoyance. She's surely dealt with difficult patients before. It must be incredibly frustrating to have your strong, capable body suddenly fail you after a traumatic accident.

"We need to keep pushing your limits," the therapist gently urges. "As a dancer, you understand that better than most. Tiny incremental progress adds up over time."

Her encouraging words trail off as Natalie's striking crystalline blue eyes meet mine across the room. I hover uncertainly in the doorway, debating whether to enter or turn back down the hall. The very air between us seems to crackle with the memory of our impulsive kiss.

As soon as Natalie's gaze locks with mine, her entire demeanor instantaneously transforms, like the sun emerging radiant from behind sullen clouds. Her taut posture noticeably relaxes against the pillows, full lips curving into a barely perceptible but alluring smile that makes my heart skip erratically.

Thankfully, the therapist remains utterly oblivious to the sudden shift, her attention still fully absorbed in the paperwork strewn across her lap. The energy in the confined room has morphed into something far softer and more intimate in mere seconds. Still, I'd die on the spot if she noticed the flush creeping up my neck or the involuntary smile teasing my lips.

I tentatively return Natalie's clandestine smile, overcome by a surge of emotions I can't begin to untangle or comprehend. Excitement, desire, fear, anticipation, and frustration are all dangerously intertwined. It seems, at the same time, forbidden and profoundly right.

The therapist absently glances up, accidentally catching Natalie's gaze still fixed intently on me. She fidgets distractedly with her pen for a moment before turning her head toward me as well.

"Ok, let's end here for today. Good work, Miss Fey," she declares abruptly. "We'll pick this up again tomorrow."

The door clicks shut behind her with an air of damning finality. I bite my lip apprehensively as a flood of embarrassment washes over me, heating my cheeks.

"OMG, you're blushing like a schoolgirl," Natalie lightly teases, though her eyes sparkle with barely restrained longing, conveying the words we both dare not speak aloud.

I know I should simply turn and flee back to the safety of the hallway outside. Instead, I am drawn inexorably to Natalie's side, as if she possessed her own gravitational field.

Natalie takes my hand in hers, lightly twining our fingers together. "I can't stop thinking about you," she whispers, her thumb slowly stroking along my knuckles.

Suddenly, my heart pounds out a frantic rhythm against my ribs. "This...this is complicated," I lamely protest. "You're my patient; I'm your doctor..."

"Shhh..." Natalie silences me by bringing her fingertips to my lips in a feather-light caress. "Let's not overthink this."

"I can't. I'm sorry," I reply, avoiding her intense gaze.

Natalie smiles softly and peppers me with questions in a rapid-fire sequence. "How was your morning? Have you eaten yet? Did you sleep alright?"

I respond in mumbled monosyllables, trying to deflect any personal details, no matter how small.

"Our kiss yesterday...it was nice, wasn't it?" she asks suddenly.

I'm sure my expression betrays the panic rising within me, as Natalie can't suppress a gentle laugh. Part of me hoped we could simply forget it happened. But, clearly, she has other plans.

"What has you so on edge?" Natalie presses. "Are you afraid to have feelings for a woman?"

"No, that's not the problem," I defend weakly.

"Then what is it?"

I wrap my arms around myself, wishing I could melt into the floor and disappear. My mind is a war zone, two voices locked in fierce debate. One reminds me of ethics, hospital policies, and professional boundaries. Natalie is my patient, the voice hisses; I must keep my distance.

But the other voice grows louder, insisting that Natalie makes me feel alive like no one else ever has, even though we only met a few days ago.

I want to give in, to explore these exhilarating free-fall feelings with her. But the voice of reason shrieks warnings, trying to protect me from my own impulses and shattered professionalism. For now, fear wins out. I cling to the rules, shutting Natalie out.

She takes a deep breath before continuing in a somber tone. "The accident was...horrific. One moment, I was speeding recklessly; the next, I was trapped in twisted metal, certain I would die."

Natalie describes the piercing pain as her leg was crushed, how she blacked out intermittently. Brief flashes of memory — firefighters using the Jaws of Life to free her limp body. Overwhelming panic. Bone-chilling fear.

Her voice wavers, and she blinks back tears recalling those first days out of her coma, her muddled mind terrified she may never walk again. It's still agonizing for her to relive. A single tear escapes down her cheek.

Instinctively, I reach for her hand, giving it a supportive squeeze. Natalie's eyes meet mine, and in them, I see relief that someone finally understands her trauma.

"Some days, I don't even know if this is real or just a horrific nightmare," Natalie confesses, averting her eyes toward the window to hide her tears. "Being trapped here, unable to move, my dancing career in jeopardy...my anxiety is through the roof."

"You'll recover, I promise," I assure her.

"Please don't. For the first time, people see me as damaged, weak...not the graceful dancer I was, able to bring an entire theater to its feet." Natalie takes a shuddering breath. "I know you mean well, but no one can guarantee I'll ever dance professionally again."

I just nod. "Considering your injuries, it's a miracle you'll live a normal life at all."

"But dancing is my normal life," Natalie replies, her voice trembling. "Not knowing if I can have that back triggers paralyzing anxiety attacks. I just want to be who I was before."

She quickly brushes away the tears streaming down her cheeks, clearly uncomfortable with this sudden openness between us.

And Arya's words echo in my mind: "When she's no longer your patient, nothing is stopping you two from being together." The prospect thrills and terrifies me, butterflies swirling wildly.

Still, seeing Natalie so distraught also breeds hesitation. We barely know each other. She's volatile, wounded. Am I ready to risk my heart if she gives me the chance?

Lost in thought, I barely notice Natalie retrieving her phone until she passes it to me. "This is all that's left of who I was," she murmurs sadly.

Natalie is unrecognizable yet achingly familiar on the tiny screen — a captivating force of nature, every movement infused with passion. I'm mesmerized, goosebumps rising as she dances with grace.

"I hope to see you perform live someday," I sigh, returning the phone.

"Watching those videos is like glimpsing another life that I may never get back." Natalie's voice catches.

I fight back tears of my own. A dancer with a broken body — could anything be more cruel?

"I'm so sorry," I whisper, and those are the only words that feel right. I clasp her hand in both of mine, wishing I could heal her with just a touch.

Natalie only nods, looking small and defeated in the stark hospital bed. But in her eyes, I see a glimmer of her indomitable spirit, a flame not yet extinguished.

She's broken but not beaten, and I'll do everything in my power to rekindle that fire.

"You're the only one who sees the real me. Not just the patient in room 305 or the dancer who can't dance anymore," Natalie says, squeezing my hand. "You make me feel alive."

An idea strikes as I lift her hand to my lips to kiss her knuckles. It's risky, but maybe with Arya's help...

"Just trust me," I say with a growing smile. "I'm going to remind you who you truly are."

Chapter 13

"So, are you in?" I prod her once more.

"For the last time, hell yes," she snaps back.

"Arya, we're going to break some rules and…"

"Breaking rules is my favorite pastime, especially when it's worth it, like now" she retorts.

"How do we pull this off?"

"You fetch your make-believe girlfriend, and I'll take care of the setup. Bring her straight there," Arya instructs, grinning from ear to ear, seemingly relishing the whole thing more than I am.

Anxiety gnaws at me as I glance at the clock again. It's nearly midnight, and the hospital seems eerily quiet tonight. My heart is a frenzied drum solo in my chest as I navigate the empty wheelchair down the dimly lit corridor.

I'm not one to cross lines. Hell, I've never had so much as a speeding ticket or a parking violation in my whole life. Now, I'm taking a significant risk; I know that. A risk that defies several hospital protocols, professional boundaries, and my own common sense. Arya assures me that no one will even notice, and that she's gotten out of stickier situations, but I'm quaking in my boots.

Ever since Natalie was admitted to this hospital, I can't shake her from my thoughts. At first, it was merely a daydream. I guess it was my escape from the day to day stress and worries. But now, it's morphed into something more, something I can't quite put a label on.

When she shared her feelings with me, it shattered my heart. I want to do something special, something that will lift her spirits, something she will remember for a long time. I yearn for Natalie to feel cherished, to rediscover that sense of joy and wonder that seems to have slipped away. I need to reignite the tiny spark that still glows within her.

I knock on her room door with trembling hands and crack it open slightly. Natalie looks at me, perplexed, stretching her arms in a languid yawn.

"Are you awake?" I whisper.

"Now I am," she replies, but her grin doesn't hint at any real complaint.

"I have a little surprise for you," I confess, edging closer to her bed.

"A wheelchair?"

"Not part of the surprise, but we'll need it to wheel you around the hospital," I explain.

"Are we escaping out of this place?" She jests, arching her eyebrows.

"Close, very close. Do you trust me?"

"Don't tell me you're giving me what I asked for a few days ago because I still need it," she teases with a playful wink.

"No, not that. But I think you'll enjoy it just the same," I assure her.

"Alright. I trust you. Anyway, anything that means getting out of this room is welcome," Natalie concedes.

With slightly more difficulty than I had anticipated, I help her onto the wheelchair and drape a blanket over her lap. It's not cold, but she's been bedridden for days. Feeling her weight lean against me is a strange sensation, enough to send a tingle down my lower abdomen despite our doing nothing more than this.

I push the wheelchair through the hallways, our gaze meeting every now and then. She smiles, her eyes wide with excitement, as if embarking on an adventure. The few night shift nurses we cross paths with give us peculiar looks, but just as Arya predicted, they go about their business without posing any questions.

Upon reaching the hospital's cafeteria, Natalie lets out a gasp of surprise. She covers her mouth with her hands, her astonishment undisguised.

I am equally stunned.

Arya has outdone herself, no doubt about that. The usually mundane and sterile space is completely transformed. At least one corner of the vast cafeteria.

On one of the tables, she's strung pastel-colored lights, casting the area in a warm, romantic glow. I'd rather not know where she got them from. Beside it, she's assembled an array of ice creams, mimicking a hastily set up ice cream parlor. She's even placed a paper sign reading "Rachel's Ice Cream Shop," adorned with a couple of colorful hearts. I could strangle her for it.

She's pulled out all the stops. There are ice creams in an array of flavors: chocolate, vanilla, strawberry, and a few more exotic ones. I plan to share them with the ER nurses when we're done, so they don't go to waste.

"Wow, this is freaking amazing!" Natalie exclaims, her hands shooting up to her head as she takes it all in.

"Told you you'd like it," I say, a hint of pride coloring my voice.

"Did you do this for me?" she asks, her smile radiant.

"Yeah, with some help, but I wanted to do something special," I admit, my heart fluttering at her reaction.

"I... I'm speechless. It's so beautiful, Rachel."

"Pick your poison," I suggest, gesturing towards the array of flavors Arya has left on the table.

Natalie ponders for a brief moment before settling on chocolate while I scoop myself a generous portion of the tart strawberry.

"I don't know if it's really this good, but right now, I'd say this is the best ice cream I've ever had," she proclaims, her eyes closing in bliss after the first bite.

For a moment, I think that even if I get caught and reprimanded, seeing Natalie's face light up like this makes it worth the risk.

"This is one of the sweetest things anyone's ever done for me," she confesses, her voice choked with emotion. "You need to try this one."

She feeds me a spoonful, and I can't tell if the ice cream tastes divine because it's genuinely good, or because the spoon was just in Natalie's mouth. Either way, I close my eyes and savor it as if it were a gourmet delicacy.

"You have no idea what I want to do to you right now," she murmurs, leaning closer and biting her lower lip.

"I think I'd prefer not to know," I sigh. "I've already broken enough rules with this ice cream stunt."

Natalie grins, and soon we're exchanging stories: childhood mischief, dreams, fears. Each tale feels like a window into our souls, offering fleeting glimpses of our innermost selves.

I tell her about the time I broke my only rule as a child, sneaking into the school kitchen to steal slices of cheesecake while evading the cook's watchful eye. How my first patient was a grumpy old man who refused his medication until I climbed onto a chair and stared him down. How my deepest fear is never finding someone who truly understands me and staying alone.

In turn, Natalie shares how she once convinced all the little ballerinas to hide when the teacher entered the studio, making her believe no one had come to class. How her first performance on Broadway had her vomiting for hours before the curtain went up. How much she fears never dancing again.

With each story, each whispered confidence, we peel away another layer of our defenses, revealing a piece of our hearts.

"I'm sorry I was so forward the other day," she suddenly admits.

"Forward? Nah, I get that all the time, believe it or not. From men and women," I quip, attempting to lighten the mood.

"I know it bothered you, and I'm sorry," she insists.

"A little."

"Is there a reason? And don't say it's because it's forbidden and all that shit, because I sense there's more to it."

I pause, thoughtful. Admitting it to Arya is one thing, but confessing that my fantasies about this woman go beyond sex to something deeper is entirely different.

"You don't want to tell me?"

"I'm not sure if I should," I admit, lowering my voice.

"I told you I wanted you to fuck me, and I'm not ashamed. I don't see how it can be worse than that," she shrugs, her smile mischievous.

"Uh, I don't even know where to begin.".

"Choose whichever path feels easiest. Or just rip it off like a band-aid," Natalie suggests, cradling my hand in hers and gently squeezing it.

"I have feelings for you," I confess, releasing a soft, shaky breath.

"Me too. What's the problem?"

"Natalie, it's not just a physical attraction I'm talking about. It's deeper. You might think it's silly, and I know I'm going to regret saying this. But when you were in a coma, those days I spent with you in ICU, I found myself picturing a life with you in vivid detail — wedding, babies, and later on. ."

"Wait, are you serious? While I was in a coma? Babies?" she interjects, her tone laced with surprise.

"Okay, I know it sounds very strange. Arya says it's unsettling, but..."

"I think it's beautiful," she cuts me off, her hands tightening around mine.

"Really?"

"Absolutely. Cross my heart," she assures me with a nod.

"The thing is, I don't want sex. Well, I do, but I want more."

"A relationship?"

"I guess that's what I'm trying to say," I sigh.

"We barely know each other."

"That's what relationships are for, right? To know each other. Even if you feel something, no one can be certain it'll work out," I explain.

"I'm not good with relationships. I always end up hurting people, or they hurt me. Or both," she admits, her gaze piercing into mine.

"I'm willing to take that risk," I assure her.

"Would it be like tonight, but every day?"

"Yeah, that's the idea."

"Too much ice cream. I would gain weight, and then surely, I couldn't dance," she deadpans.

"No, I didn't mean…"

"I know, silly. It's tempting," Natalie concedes.

"But right now, it's impossible. You know, hospital rules and all," I explain.

"So, just for tonight… let's pretend."

I nod and shrug my shoulders. If only I could fast-forward time until Natalie is discharged. I want to break down the walls she's erected to protect herself, even if it means doing it brick by brick.

We've been alone during these stolen hours from sleep, sharing laughter, dreams, and ice cream. It's time to return her to her room, and my mind is a swarm of thoughts, buzzing with possibilities. A million thoughts crowd my mind, but one stands out: I don't want this night to end.

"Sweet dreams, get some rest, beautiful," I whisper before turning off the lights and leaving her room..

Chapter 14

"Whoa, you look like something the cat dragged in!" Arya announces, eyeing me as I shuffle toward our table in the hospital cafeteria.

A steaming mug of double-strength coffee rests on the table before me as I try, unsuccessfully, to mask a yawn that could swallow the world. Sleep was elusive last night, a slippery creature that darted in and out of reach.

"You seem to be desperate for caffeine. Is that a sign the date went well?" Arya asks, leaning forward with a mischievous arch of her brows.

I shrug, releasing a sigh that's heavy with exhaustion and uncertainty as I scramble for words. How do I define something that I'm still struggling to comprehend?

"You know it wasn't a date, right?" I counter weakly, though I doubt my protest has any effect on Arya's teasing.

"Just keep telling yourself that, darling," she retorts, her voice laced with playful sarcasm. "So, did she like the ice cream surprise?"

"She loved it. I think it meant a lot to her, and I appreciate you going all out to create such a romantic atmosphere," I admit, my lips curving into a grateful smile.

"And was it enough to...you know..." Arya trails off, her fingers making an obscene gesture.

"God, you're crude."

"Is that a yes?" she persists, her eyes sparkling with curiosity.

"No, Arya. It's totally against the rules, and it's insane that you, as head of surgery, would even ask," I scold, my hands flitting up to cradle my aching head.

"Are you going to spill the details about your non-date or not? Please, at least tell me you two kissed under those lights I set up. It took me forever to find them."

I shake my head, squinting at her in disbelief, even as a blush blooms on my cheeks. The memory of how close we came to that kiss Arya is so desperate to hear about sends a jolt through me.

"OK, where do I start? We made it to the cafeteria without a hitch, just like you said. No kiss, but we had this...this beautiful conversation. We opened up to each other in a way we hadn't before. But when I left her in her room, I felt this...emptiness, like something was missing," I confess, a sigh slipping past my lips.

"Oh là là, love is in the air!" Arya exclaims, her voice soaring and drawing the attention of a group of nurses at a nearby table. "Tell me more, please."

"And you lower your voice. The last thing I need is for my boss to get wind of this," I plead, my eyes darting around to make sure we haven't attracted a crowd.

Arya apologizes, theatrically clapping her hands over her mouth, and promises to whisper from now on.

"I told her, while visiting her in the ICU... I'd talk to her, picturing us married, with kids, and..."

"You didn't!" Arya exclaims, a mouthful of coffee threatening to spray across the table. "Please, tell me you're joking."

"I'm dead serious. I spilled my guts, and she was incredibly understanding. She said it was very tender," I assure her.

"Damn, you cheeky thing. I can't believe you told the ballerina about your fantasies of marrying her and having babies. That's disturbing, even by my standards," she interrupts, wiping tears of laughter from her eyes.

"OK, when you put it that way, it does sound a bit odd."

"Because it is odd. But, sorry, go on, don't let me interrupt," Arya urges.

"I ended up telling her my feelings for her and..."

"Are you two going to start dating?" she interrupts again.

"She didn't say yes or no. She simply mentioned her bad luck with relationships and how she usually ends up hurting the other person or herself," I explain.

"So, are we talking just sex, then?"

"Could you let me finish, for God's sake?" I protest. "We didn't discuss that."

"So, what's the plan now?"

"I guess to keep spending time with her until she's discharged, then try to see her outside the hospital once she's no longer my patient. She'll be in a cast and in recovery for a while, so she'll need help."

"Promise me I'll be your bridesmaid when you marry her," she declares, winking mischievously.

"You're such an idiot, but if it happens, I promise."

Arya pumps her fists in victory, and I can't help but roll my eyes. She always manages to lift my spirits, no matter how tired I am. Suddenly, I guess, by comparison, my boss crosses my mind.

"Anything wrong?" Arya asks, noticing my expression shift.

"Can I tell you something in confidence? It's eating me alive, and if I don't tell someone, I feel like my head will explode," I confess, avoiding her eye. "I don't want to drag you into this, but you're the only person I trust entirely."

"You know you can tell me anything," Arya assures me.

"Just promise me you won't do anything rash."

"Rash?"

"Without consulting me first because I know what you're about to hear is not going to sit well with you, and I know you," I warn her.

"Alright," she agrees, raising her hand as if she's on a witness stand.

"It's about Richard, my boss," I start, lowering my voice to a barely audible whisper.

"That jerk?"

"He's more than just a jerk," I sigh heavily, the weight of it all pressing down on my chest.

"How so?"

"Ever since I started working in his department, I've felt harassed. At first, it was just inappropriate comments that made me uncomfortable. Then he suggested we should go out for dinner. Later, he proposed we sleep together while his wife was away, and…"

"That fucking pig!" Arya interrupts, her face a harsh mask of tension.

"Yeah, but there's more," I reluctantly admit.

"More?" she echoes, shock lacing her voice.

"Much more. At one point, he confessed to fantasizing about me, and... he even brushed himself against me," I stammer, nerves making my words stumble.

"Damn it! That son of a bitch... I swear, I'll rip his head off," Arya declares, her body shaking with rage.

"You promised you wouldn't act on your own," I remind her.

"This can't stand, Rachel. Do you have any witnesses?"

"The issue is that my only witness is Natalie, and I don't want to drag her into this mess," I confess, my fingers twisting restlessly.

"Natalie?"

"It happened during a shift. Late one night. Richard thought she was asleep, and he became very aggressive. Natalie heard everything and confronted him. Since then, I haven't faced any issues, but I can't help feeling on edge every time I see him. I avoid being alone with my boss at all costs. I've even had a few panic attacks," I confess, lowering my gaze.

"Wow, I've got a whole new respect for Natalie! I love that she stood up to him."

"I know I should report him to Human Resources, but you know his connections. His father-in-law is on the hospital's Board of Directors."

"From what I've heard, his father-in-law can't stand him," Arya counters. "He put him in charge of ER, and Richard is utterly incompetent."

"I don't know if I can handle going through all of that, Arya. Reliving it in front of HR... just thinking about it makes me shiver," I admit. "And if it's all for nothing, I don't know if I could handle it. Plus, I don't want to drag Natalie back into this. Things have been calm for a few days, thanks to her."

"But think about the other women," Arya interrupts. "Even if he never tries anything with you again, you're likely not the only one. Other young women in the same situation might be too afraid to report for the same reason. Residents, nurses... Richard needs to be stopped before it continues."

"I know, I know, but please, let me think it over."

"I have another idea. It's safer for you. Unless you're the only one he's harassing, which I doubt," Arya suddenly blurts out, her eyes lighting up as if a lightbulb has just switched on in her mind.

Chapter 15

The conversation about Richard leaves me rattled. I know Arya is right, even if it's a particularly uncomfortable circumstance for me. We need to stop him somehow. We can't let him get away with such blatant harassment. I must do it not only for myself but also for other potential victims. I'm sure they exist, and if we do nothing to prevent it, there will be more in the future.

However, it's far easier said than done. The issue with these situations is that we women have to relive something that made us feel incredibly uncomfortable over and over again.

It'll be his word against mine. Even if we bring Natalie as a witness, I know they will do everything possible to paint me as a liar or worse. They'll likely try to make it seem like I was the one who initiated all the trouble.

The morning is dragging on, what with my exhaustion and doubts about Richard. The only bright spot is my visit to Natalie, which brightens my face with a smile.

A smile that evaporates as quickly as it had appeared as soon as I enter her room.

I find her sitting on the edge of the bed, her gaze lost on some far-off point through the window. She's got her elbows dug into her knees, and her whole body shudders with each sob.

My blood runs cold at the sight of her. I approach cautiously, drawn by an unstoppable need to fold her into an embrace and comfort her. As she senses my presence, she briefly glances my way, her beautiful eyes now filled with tears. A fresh sob tears at my heart.

"Natalie, are you okay?" I whisper, concern seeping through.

Hearing her name, she shakes her head but doesn't look at me. She wipes away the tears streaking her cheeks with her hand, and my breath catches at her sadness.

I sit next to her, leaving a few inches between us. I want to respect her space but also invite her to trust me and share what's happening.

"What happened?" I press.

For a moment, my mind buzzes with possibilities. I imagine all sorts of devastating news that could've happened. She opens her mouth a couple of times, her lower lip trembling as she struggles to form words, to give voice to the turmoil within.

When she finally manages to speak, her voice comes out choked and weak.

"It's over, Rachel. Everything I've worked for since I was a child... it's over. All of it. I'll never dance again."

New tears spill down her cheeks. Dance is everything to her. It's her passion, her purpose, the very core of her identity. It could all be cut short now because of that tragic accident.

"I don't see any new entries in your medical history. Have you spoken with the trauma surgeons?" I ask, fear creeping in.

I wish I could somehow absorb some of her pain, but I don't even know what's happening. So, I simply take her hand, our fingers interlacing, offering silent support in the face of the unknown.

"I haven't spoken to any doctors, but I know it. My world's shrunk to this tiny hospital room. Four walls closing in on me, a little more each day, suffocating me. Our midnight ice cream run was nice, Rachel, but it's nothing more than a mirage. When I look at myself in the bathroom mirror, I barely recognize myself. My body feels foreign, alien. I move awkwardly, not a trace of the dancer I once was."

"You can't know that. Not you, not anyone, because it relies on so many factors. The trauma surgeons say your progress is stellar. We need to wait a few weeks, see how you keep improving with physical therapy, and keep hope alive. Everything may turn out okay. I firmly believe that," I assure her, leaning in to press a kiss against her cheek.

I gently rub her back, tasting the salty tang of her tears on my lips. I hate to give hope without facts. It could go wrong, and it feels like a lie. But right now, I don't know what else I could do to lift her spirits.

Natalie shakes her head with a grimace of bitterness and shifts her gaze away from mine.

"Dance is the only language I know. It's how I've expressed myself since I was a kid. The thought of losing it terrifies me. I fear that I'll lose myself, not only my body but also my whole identity. Each time I imagine not dancing again, it feels like I'm being buried alive. It's a crushing, devastating feeling. It's horrible to watch all your dreams fade away," she breathes out, her voice hitching.

"No matter what happens, I'm here for you. You know that, right?" I reassure her, drawing small circles on her palm with my thumb.

A hint of a smile, ghost-like, flickers on her lips for the briefest second. She squeezes my hand tightly, trying to communicate what her words can't.

"I'm glad you're here, Rachel," she whispers, piercing me with her gaze for the first time since I walked into her room. "You might not believe it, but sometimes, you're the only thing keeping me sane."

I embrace her, and as if pulled by gravity, her face drifts closer to mine. I know I should pull back, but I find myself frozen, suspended in this moment. It's as if the room itself is holding its breath, everything moving in slow motion.

The tip of her nose brushes against mine, our lips meet in a brief but electrifying touch, and when I feel one of her hands circle my neck, I pull away abruptly, the spell broken.

My heart pounds so hard it threatens to burst from my chest. To say that I want to kiss her is an understatement, but I can't let it happen.

"I'm sorry, I shouldn't have done that," she mutters, noticing my trembling form.

"I think I should leave," I announce.

"Don't you trust me?"

"Right now, I don't trust myself, Natalie," I admit, trying to catch my breath.

She nods, but I see a glint of disappointment in her eyes, though I know she understands that there are lines I can't cross. At least, not at the moment.

"I'll come by tomorrow to check on you, okay? If you need to talk, this is my cell phone," I say as I write down my number on a piece of paper.

"Thank you for everything you do for me," Natalie says, watching me leave the room.

Arya

I've never been one to shy away from a challenging conversation, but this one's got my palms slick with sweat.

Ever since Rachel confessed Richard's harassment to me, I've been climbing the walls. Hell, I even struggled to focus in the OR today. That bastard! I'd love to take a scalpel to him.

I get why Rachel's torn about reporting him. He's her boss, well-connected, but this has to stop. For her sake and for other potential victims, which I'm certain he's got in his past and will have in his future unless we do something about it.

The dancer, Natalie, is the only direct witness, so I have to talk to her despite Rachel's plea not to. I need to know exactly what happened and if she'd be willing to testify against that son of a bitch.

"Come in," she invites as soon as she catches sight of me peeking through the door.

She's seated on the bed, engrossed in the view out the window. The woman is stunning. No wonder Rachel's smitten. Her hair, piled up in a messy bun, lends her a delicate air. It's hard to imagine she put Richard in his place.

"You're one of the trauma surgeons?" she inquires, opening her eyes wide.

"No, I'm a cardiac surgeon."

"Cardiac surgeon?" she echoes, surprised.

"No, no, easy there," I hasten to clarify, "I'm not here to operate or anything. Just relax. I'm a friend of Rachel's, Arya Kumari."

"Oh, the ice cream lady? Rachel talks about you a lot."

"Only terrible things, I'm sure," I joke, letting myself sink into the chair by her bed.

She smiles, and it's a beautiful one. It's clearer than ever why Rachel's lost in her.

"Listen, I need to discuss something with you, something delicate. I'm not the best with these types of conversations. I tend to be a bit blunt," I warn her upfront.

"Go ahead."

"It's about Rachel's boss."

"That pig," she mutters, clicking her tongue in disgust.

"Exactly, he's a total jerk. We agree on that," I assure her. "But he can't get away with this. Rachel told me you witnessed it and even confronted him."

"That's correct. The way he treated Rachel is unacceptable. That man is detestable. He shouldn't be working in this hospital," Natalie asserts, her teeth gritted.

"There's no debate there, but Rachel's unsure about reporting him to HR. Not only is he her boss, but his father-in-law is on the Board of Directors, though from what I've heard, he's fed up with him, too. The next issue is, you're a crucial piece of this puzzle, although Rachel insists on keeping you out of it and…"

"I have no problem about testifying if she decides to report him," she interrupts me. "That man can't be allowed to abuse his power. I understand her hesitation, though."

"Exactly! We need to take that fucking bastard down!" I blurt out, my voice louder than intended.

Judging by her expression, I've taken her by surprise, so I attempt to calm myself down a bit. I don't want to scare her off. She doesn't seem easily intimidated, though.

"It's not just about Rachel, dire as that may be. We must stop him from exploiting more young women who rely on him," I articulate, my words hanging heavy in the sterile hospital air.

"Yeah, I'm in," Natalie declares without hesitation. "Just tell me what you need from me. Consider me at your disposal," she adds, her voice resolute and unwavering.

"Thank you," I whisper, my fingers offering a gentle squeeze on her shoulder, the crisp fabric of her hospital gown crinkling beneath my touch. "I needed to know if I could count on you when the time comes. However, I've thought of a strategy that might spare both you and Rachel the brunt of it. At the very least, it'd prevent you two from being the only ones to lock horns with Richard."

Her eyebrows furrow in confusion, "I'm not sure I follow."

"In India, they trap monkeys with a container that has a tiny opening. Inside, they put a fruit or something the monkey likes. When the monkey reaches in and grabs the food, it can't pull its hand out unless it lets go of the treat. Their instincts are their downfall," I explain, my eyes locked with hers.

"Is Richard the monkey in this scenario?"

"More or less... His instincts and the belief that he's untouchable will also be his downfall. We'll set a trap he won't be able to deny," I announce, a spark of determination igniting in my core.

"I'm all ears," Natalie exclaims, a grin spreading from ear to ear.

"Before we dive into that, can I doodle something on your cast, please? It's an odd compulsion I've had since I was a kid. I see a blank cast, and I'm compelled to sketch something, to inject some life into its dull surface," I confess, pointing at her cast devoid of any traces of drawings or signatures.

Natalie shrugs in amusement. Meanwhile, I pour my limited artistic talent into creating something emblematic.

"Two ice creams surrounded by tiny hearts?" she questions, a soft chuckle escaping her lips.

"Yeah, only the three of us will know the meaning," I remind her with a playful wink.

Chapter 16

Arya teases that I'm grinning like a fool. To quote her, more like an idiot, but today Natalie gets discharged. The terror of those initial days when we had to keep her in a medically induced coma after the horrifying accident feels distant now. After fearing she might endure lasting damage, she's going home with only a broken leg. Her body has fought, and triumphed.

From the doorway of her room, I watch her hurriedly stuff her last belongings into a duffel bag. Her movements are quick and strained, her brow creased, as if she can't get out of here fast enough.

I don't blame her. Being confined to a hospital for as long as she has must be suffocating. The constant intrusions by doctors and nurses at all hours, the fear of an uncertain recovery. It's no place for rest or joy.

"Need a hand with anything?" I ask, closing the distance between us with measured steps.

Natalie pauses and gifts me a radiant smile.

"I've got everything, thank you," she assures me, her hand brushing gently against my left arm.

"I'm thrilled you're finally discharged. You've made a remarkable recovery these past weeks. How does it feel to be leaving here after all this time?" I query, settling beside her on the bed.

"Excitement, joy. But also nerves and panic," she confesses with a nonchalant shrug. "In a way, the hospital is a safe space. Everything is monitored; there's always someone taking care of me. But out there…" Her voice trails off as she casts a glance at the bustling New York through the window.

"Everything will be all right, you'll see," I interject, clasping her hand in mine. "Before you know it, you'll be fully healed and dancing. Just promise me you'll take things slow and not push yourself too hard. Your leg needs to heal at its own pace. You can't rush it," I remind her, giving her hand a reassuring squeeze.

"I know. Patience has never been my strong suit, but I'll try," she responds, her lips curving into a smile.

We chat for a while like two old friends. I ask her how she feels about sleeping in her own bed again, cooking again, and seeing her neighborhood again. Her excitement seems to grow with each word, and I can almost see the images taking shape in her mind.

Suddenly, we fall into silence. It's an odd hush, broken when Natalie clears her throat, and her expression turns solemn.

"I guess this is our goodbye," she sighs.

"Don't say that, please," I stammer.

Her words hit me like a cold shower as if a grand house of cards loses its delicate balance and collapses. The realization that I'll miss her mesmerizing blue eyes, that beautiful smile that could light up a small town, our talks, our good mornings and goodnights, our friendship, crashes over me.

"It doesn't have to be a farewell," I quickly clarify, my words tumbling out in a rush. "These coming days, you'll need help. I'd love to, you know, swing by your place, help with groceries, meal prep, whatever you need."

Natalie's eyes widen in surprise.

"Wow, you don't have to do that. You already work so much at the hospital," she retorts.

"I don't mind," I persist. "I would be happy to. I'd feel much better knowing I can support you as your leg recovers."

The mere thought of spending more time with her sends my heart into an excited flutter. I can almost see the conflict written across her face as she chews on her lower lip in deep thought.

"I don't want to be a burden to you," she finally says.

"You could never be a burden," I assure her, my voice barely above a whisper.

Her smile is the kind that could stop your heart.

"If you're going to give me those puppy-dog eyes, I guess I'll have to say yes. I suppose a little help would be nice," she concedes.

"Now that you're no longer my patient, I'm not letting you go that easy," I confess, wrapping her in a comforting embrace.

"Does that include what I asked you that night?" she teases.

"You're such a fool, Natalie Fey," I whisper before kissing her cheek.

The clearing of a nurse's throat pulls us from our bubble. I can feel the blush creeping up to the tips of my ears, even as she smiles and offers to return later.

"I'll take her to the exit door," I announce, searching for an excuse to steal a few more moments with Natalie.

On the sidewalk, in front of her taxi, neither of us seems eager to end this moment. But the impatient taxi driver points to his watch, hinting that he has other places to be.

"I'll see you tonight, right after my shift at the hospital," I remind her.

"Tonight," Natalie echoes, her smile radiant.

I stand there, transfixed, watching the taxi disappear into the distance, Natalie's hand waving goodbye from the rear window.

And suddenly, tonight seems like an eternity away. Her absence leaves a strange void. She just left, and I already miss her.

As I head back to the ER, I imagine what it would be like to touch her bare skin, to feel the heat of her body, the texture of her breasts against mine. I imagine making love to her all night, trembling under her touch, my...

"Did you hear the news, you dumbass?"

"Damn it, Arya! You scared me," I protest, clutching my heart.

"I need you in my office. Now," she adds.

"Your office? What's going on?" I question, a thread of unease weaving through my words.

"You'll see," Arya responds cryptically, her stride long and determined as she navigates the hospital corridor.

I trail behind her, nerves prickling beneath my skin. She's unnaturally serious today; not a shred of her usual jovial demeanor in sight.

Upon opening her office door, I'm met with two other doctors. One, a young woman around my age, is strikingly beautiful. The other, a few years older, I vaguely recall from Arya's wife's birthday party.

"This is Jackie Stone and her girlfriend, Sarah," Arya introduces.

"We met at Patricia's birthday party, didn't we?" I offer, attempting to break the ice.

"Yes, we were talking about…" Sarah begins, but Arya, in her typical brusque manner, cuts in.

"Enough with the pleasantries. Let's get down to business," she interrupts, a characteristic I'm slowly growing accustomed to.

"She's a nightmare, but we love her anyway," Doctor Stone quips, rolling her eyes dramatically.

"You really have no idea, do you?" Arya presses.

"No."

"Well, then, you must be the only one in this damn hospital who doesn't know. I'm guessing you've been too wrapped up in Natalie's world… But let's focus," she pauses, pulling a face. "We've taken care of your little problem. Well, little is an understatement…"

"My problem?"

"That fucking bastard boss of yours," Arya clarifies.

"What have you done?" I ask, fear creeping into my voice as my body starts to tremble.

"Calm down! You're not getting involved unless you want to back the cause. Which you should," she adds.

"Are you going to tell me, or do you want me to have a heart attack?" I interject, teetering on the edge of a nervous breakdown.

"You've got Sarah to thank. She played the bait. You know, the best way to catch a predator is to lay out the most irresistible bait. And Sarah is… damn…"

"Arya, for God's sake, I'm right here!" Jackie protests, but a small giggle escapes from Sarah.

"I'm still lost," I confess.

"Watch the video," she directs, pointing at her computer screen.

I can't believe what unfolds before my eyes. Richard, in his office, door closed, that sickening smile on his face that he wears when he's about to get what he wants.

He's dangerously close to a woman, caressing her arm. The woman tells him to back off, to stop, but he persists. He promises her a permanent position at the hospital once her residency is complete if she sleeps with him. His hand drifts to her waist, he tries to kiss her…

The tension in the room crackles like a live wire as I watch the scene playing out on Arya's screen. The blend of shock, relief, and a strange sense of vindication is a cocktail that leaves my head reeling.

"And the look on his face when Sarah tells him she's recording… Priceless," I murmur, still wrapped in shock.

"Holy shit! Richard nearly had a heart attack!" Arya cackles, her laughter echoing in the room.

"He even turned blue. Look at that panic-stricken face," Jackie Stone adds, her voice rich with amusement.

"But how? How did you do this?" I stammer, still struggling to accept the reality unfolding before me.

"Enter Oscar-worthy actress, Sarah," Arya explains. "We suspected Richard was trying his luck with any young woman he could isolate, so we used a pediatric patient's emergency as a chance to get her alone with him. The jerk wasted no time in taking her to his office to discuss the child's case and shut the door. The rest, you've seen. He tried his usual tricks; what he didn't know was that Sarah was recording everything with a hidden camera, streaming it directly to my phone via the hospital's WiFi."

"That's... intense," I manage to utter.

"The whole hospital knows by now. Stories of residents and nurses he harassed, leveraging his position of power, are surfacing. He's a fucking pig. It would be best if you came forward with your case, too, but either way, he's getting what he deserves. The hospital's Board of Directors is convening an emergency meeting today, and rumors are that his father-in-law is pulling strings to not only get him fired but also revoke his medical license. A predator like him shouldn't be allowed to practice."

"There's also the question of whether any of the victims want to pursue criminal charges," Dr. Stone adds. "Apparently, there have been some severe cases."

"You're... you're incredible," I assure them, tears glistening on my cheeks as I wipe them away with the back of my hand.

"We have to look out for each other," Sarah says, her voice softened by empathy.

"I don't know how I can ever thank you," I choke out, a flood of relief and gratitude washing over me.

"Now, let's focus on your future. Have you made any plans with the gorgeous dancer yet?" Arya asks, raising her eyebrows in anticipation. The tension in the room eases, replaced by a wave of lightheartedness that makes me feel like I can finally breathe again.

Chapter 17

Unwittingly, Richard becomes the talk of the town — the hospital, to be precise. The chatter is incessant; even our patients crave the juicy details during our rounds.

In an unexpected twist, Arya becomes our live correspondent during the Board meeting, sending us quick text updates as we huddle in the cafeteria. Around us, a crowd gathers, comprising nurses and residents who have been on the receiving end of Richard's twisted tyranny.

"Richard's father-in-law looks like he's about to breathe fire every time he opens his mouth," Arya's text reads. The highlight, though, is when Richard's wife storms the Board meeting to slap him right across his stunned face.

The image of my former boss, escorted out of the hospital by security guards, his life packed into a cardboard box, will forever be etched in my memory. Losing his medical license seems inevitable now. That could be just the tip of the iceberg if some of his victims push for criminal charges, as rumored.

For once, karma has been swift and just.

Despite Arya's pleas for a celebratory dinner, my feet take me straight to Natalie's place after work. The dim light of the evening bathes Manhattan in a warm, amber glow as I make my way to her apartment.

It's an odd sensation. I pause at the foot of the steps leading up to her building — a six-story brick structure nestled in the heart of Brooklyn.

I take a deep breath, smooth my shirt with trembling hands, and hoist the bags of groceries before venturing into the lobby. A tidal wave of thoughts crashes over me as I press the buzzer.

The faint chime rings out from within her apartment, and my heart skips a beat as her voice echoes through the intercom.

"Just a minute," she calls out, her voice a mechanical reflex. I know her 'just a minute' will stretch longer than she'd like. She had texted earlier about her clumsy struggles on crutches. As I wait, I wind a loose curl around my index finger, a futile attempt to keep the bubbling anticipation at bay.

"You're here!" Natalie exclaims, her smile radiant as morning sunshine. The crutch clatters to the floor as she wraps her arms around me.

"Of course, I am. I brought some food and a few other things that I thought you might need." I quickly add, noticing her surprised expression, "And I've got my PJs and toothbrush, too. Don't worry, I can sleep anywhere. Even the couch is just fine."

"You're such an angel," she murmurs. "Can you take the grocery bags to the kitchen? Crutches aren't as easy as they look," she adds apologetically.

As I navigate through the living room towards the kitchen, I can't help but pause to take in the walls. Broadway posters mingle with framed photos of Natalie in mid-performance or with some celebrity. An impressive vinyl record collection rests beside a small table. Crystal prisms dangle from a window, casting rainbow specks across the wooden floor.

Her passion for dance is evident in every corner of the apartment.

"Thank you for this, Rachel," she whispers, her hand gently caressing my back as she joins me. "You might not think it's much, but you can't imagine what it means to me."

"It's nothing," I assure her with a smile.

"It is. It's everything. You make me feel…I don't know…cherished, I guess."

"I'd like to stay at your place for a while as you recover. It's even closer to the hospital," I add, hoping to lighten the mood. "It will make your recovery easier."

She doesn't answer, but the way she shrugs and smiles simply melts my heart.

Soon, we're in the kitchen, discussing our favorite recipes and chopping vegetables for dinner. As I cut the carrots, Natalie teases me about my lackluster knife skills.

"Let me show you how it's done," she insists, reaching out to guide me.

Before I can protest, her hand gently covers mine, holding the knife handle while her other hand rests on my thigh. I feel every inch of our skin contact and a sudden flutter in my stomach.

Her chin rests lightly on my shoulder, guiding my hand as we slice through the carrots. I'm so nervous that I can't even check if the slices look better or worse than before.

"I thought you knew how to cook," she whispers in my ear, sending a chill down my spine.

Something as mundane as slicing a carrot together feels exciting and natural, an intimate dance between us. I'm only aware of the rhythmic motion of her hand guiding mine, her breath on my neck. And for some reason, it feels more sensual than anything I've done in a long time.

"Does it turn you on to cut a carrot?" Natalie hisses against my ear before gently biting my earlobe.

I don't answer her, but the involuntary sigh that escapes my mouth says more than a thousand words.

I watch as her lips arch into a subtle smile, and the knife stops moving under our hands. As I turn to look at her, I lose myself in the blue of her eyes and it's as if the atmosphere between us is charged with electricity.

She leans in slightly to kiss my lips. It's just a touch. Soft, tentative, intoxicating. She bites my lower lip, and my whole body trembles with excitement.

I wrap my arms around her neck as her hands rest on my shoulders. Natalie tangles her fingers in my hair, and I pull her body, drawing her to me.

I stroke her back, lifting her shirt to feel the softness of her skin.

"Sit on me, this cast sucks, and I can barely move," Natalie proposes, her eyes full of desire.

Breathing heavily, I straddle her legs, and our lips merge in a beautiful kiss. Soon, her mouth leaves mine to trace a path along my jaw, down my neck to reach my collarbone, which she traces with the tip of her tongue, making me shiver.

Natalie slides her fingers under my shirt, caressing my belly with the back of her hand, before gently removing it. And as soon as she unhooks the hook of my bra, freeing my boobs, she runs her fingers over my skin with such intensity that if I weren't sitting on her, I'm sure I'd lose my balance.

I fumble awkwardly with the buttons of her blouse in a vain attempt to get it off as soon as possible, though my whole body trembles with anticipation every time my fingers brush the curve of her tits.

Natalie sneaks down to the button of my jeans, unbuttoning it to caress my pubis, drawing an involuntary moan from my mouth at the feel of her fingers so close to my sex.

"Shit, the oven," she protests suddenly.

"Dinner…"

"Fuck dinner, I can't wait any longer," she exclaims between gasps.

"I agree," I joke. But let me at least turn off the oven.

Natalie sighs as I get up, though soon, her eyes light up with a new flame.

"Help me to my bedroom. We'll be more comfortable in bed," she proposes.

Once in her room, she instructs me to lie on my back, and her lips linger on my nipples, flicking them with the tip of her tongue or biting them between her lips. She barely manages to get down to my navel, which she fills with kisses before maneuvering with difficulty to caress the inside of my thighs, tracing invisible drawings with her fingers.

"I swear," Natalie moans again, pausing for a few moments.

"Let me do it! You lie down on the bed," I suggest with a wink.

"Just know that under normal conditions, I'm very dominant in sex," she jokes.

"These are not normal conditions, so you'll have to let me be the one in charge for the moment," I tell her as I take off her clothes.

We remove each of her clothes with more difficulty than expected because of the plaster cast. I try to compensate with kisses and caresses, and each of her moans transports me to paradise.

"Are you ready?" I ask when we only have to get rid of her panties.

"I've been ready since before you came to my house," Natalie sighs, lifting her hips.

I put my thumbs under the elastic of her panties and slowly slide them down until she's completely naked.

Natalie spreads her legs, and as I look closely at her sex, I can't help but let out a long sigh. I pull her lips slightly apart, her glistening with arousal.

Reaching out, I stroke her pubis as I move closer and closer to her. And there, positioned between her legs, as I slowly slide my tongue along her sex, with Natalie moaning in pleasure, I know I'm with the one I'm meant to be with.

As I fiddle with her clit, making her whole body tense, I slip two of my fingers inside her. I finger her slowly, feeling the heat and wetness of her arousal on every millimeter of my skin, our moans intermingling.

"Give me your fingers," she orders with bated breath.

I sit up slightly and move closer to her. Natalie takes my hand, and my heart does a somersault the moment she slips my fingers, still wet, into her mouth, moaning as she savors her own arousal.

"Go back to fucking me," she orders.

And that slight dominant touch in her voice makes me shudder.

I slip my fingers back inside her as I rub my sex over her leg with each thrust. Our hips move in unison, our breathing ragged.

"Fuck, Rachel," she sighs between moans.

"Touch yourself while I fuck you!" I whisper.

Natalie smiles and starts stroking her clit with her fingertips. And the sensation of watching her masturbate from inches away while I continue to make love to her is sublimely sensual.

She comes undone with moans. Her legs tremble as I rub myself on one of them harder and harder, mad with desire, feeling an orgasm building inside me without even touching myself.

"Fuck!" she squeals, abandoning herself on the mattress and bringing both hands to her head.

"Did you like it?" I ask as I try to catch my breath.

"Should I answer? You don't know how much I wanted to. Why did you stop? You were about to, weren't you?" Natalie asks, combing my hair between her fingers.

"I was, but, I don't know, it felt weird to keep rubbing myself on your leg when you'd already had an orgasm," I explain.

"You're silly," Natalie whispers, kissing my forehead. Now I want you to lie down next to me and finish it while looking into my eyes," she adds with a look full of desire.

"Are you serious?"

"Totally serious," she assures me in a whisper.

And while I get lost in the primal passion of those beautiful blue eyes, I must admit that touching myself next to her, enjoying that intimate moment for her, is the most exciting thing I've ever done in my life.

Chapter 18

"I've got a surprise for you," I whisper into Natalie's ear as the morning sun peeks through our window.

Her eyes flutter open, still heavy with sleep, her head nestled on my chest. Those expressive blue eyes, which I've already fallen head over heels for, fixate on me, full of curiosity.

"A surprise?" she mumbles.

"We might need to hustle, though. I know we didn't catch much sleep, but..."

"And, who's fault is that?" she teases, her voice still thick.

"Mutual culpability, I'd say. But now, get up and get dressed. We've got places to be," I reply, giving her a playful wink.

"We're going somewhere?"

"I've set up a romantic date for us. I know it's a bit unorthodox to have sex before our first official date, but I suppose neither of us was in the mood for restraint," I admit.

"We can consider the ice cream escapade in the hospital as our first date. That way, it isn't so odd. Plus, we have Arya's artwork as evidence," she suggests, pointing towards the drawing etched onto her plaster cast.

"That works for me. Now, up and at 'em, we're burning daylight!" I urge.

"In case you've forgotten, I'm rather limited with this cast and a broken leg," she reminds me, a hint of frustration in her eyes as she gestures towards her wrapped right leg.

"I've got it all figured out," I assure her, pressing a soft kiss onto her forehead.

With a skeptical expression, Natalie squints and shakes her head, amusement dancing in her eyes. I'm growing fond of her expressive gaze, her animated gestures. Maybe that's a part of her allure on the dance floor.

When we step outside, a cab is waiting by her apartment. I give the driver instructions in hushed tones, hoping to keep our destination a secret. Natalie's face lights up with curiosity.

"Are you going to give me a hint?" she prods, resting her head on my shoulder and tracing her fingers lightly over my thigh.

"It's something special. That's all I'm saying."

"Intriguing... but I deserve something special," she purrs, nuzzling into my neck.

"I know,"

When the cab pulls up on 59th Street, her eyes widen.

"Wait, please don't tell me that..."

Before she can finish, I press a finger to her lips. Ahead of us, a handsome dappled horse stands patiently, harnessed to an elegant carriage with plush burgundy seats.

"You've got to be kidding me. Are we really going on a horse-drawn carriage ride? Through Central Park?" she asks, disbelief lacing her voice.

"Have you ever done it before?"

"Never."

"Me neither. It always seemed so romantic, and with your cast, it's the best date idea I could think of," I confess.

"Well, you've nailed it," she admits, raising her eyebrows and biting her lip.

A man in his fifties tips his hat in greeting and waves us aboard. It's not the easiest task with Natalie's broken leg, but once she's settled in, she looks as thrilled as a child tasting chocolate for the first time.

Once we are ready, the driver clicks his tongue and flicks the reins, setting the massive horse in motion. We move at a steady pace, the majestic brownstone buildings passing by. The rhythmic clip-clop of the horse's hooves against the cobblestones is like a lullaby.

"This is truly incredible," Natalie admits, snuggled into my shoulder.

"I wanted it to be something we'd remember forever."

"Forever?" she questions, arching an eyebrow. "That's a very long time."

"Don't ruin the date," I murmur, brushing a kiss against her hair.

"You're so silly! You know? I'm contemplating the idea of giving you a chance, in case you hadn't noticed."

Soon, the rhythmic clatter of wheels and the horse's occasional neighs fade. The city's clamor dissolves, and all that's left is Natalie, nestled sweetly against me. We share a tender kiss every so often, as we pass the park's iconic landmarks.

The morning wind whips around us, rustling the leaves on the trees like a thousand tiny whispers.

"It feels like we have all of Central Park to ourselves," she sighs, leaning in to plant another kiss on my lips.

"Just wait until you see the view of the lake in this light. It's breathtaking," I promise her.

Natalie's been in New York for sixteen years, and I was born here. Yet, we marvel at every detail as though we're a pair of tourists who've just landed, pointing out secret statues, bridges, and the lush path our carriage traverses.

As we veer off the main path, the lake greets us, shimmering as it catches the morning sunlight. Natalie's jaw drops, and she squeezes my hand.

"I've lived in this city for years, and I've never seen it look this beautiful," she admits.

"It might be the company."

"You're such a goof!" she murmurs, a playful squint in her eyes.

Regrettably, our forty-five-minute ride ends too soon. But judging by the smile etched on Natalie's lips, it's been worth it.

"Don't let it go to your head, Dr. Harris, but this might be the best date of my life. You're making quite a case for a serious relationship," she teases, her eyes twinkling with a flirtatious wink.

***

Nestled into the worn cushions of her apartment sofa, we try to pay attention to the flickering television screen. It's a losing battle against the electricity coursing between us, distracting us with an intoxicating rhythm of stolen kisses and gentle caresses.

"What's wrong?" I ask as her face drains of its prior lightness, replaced by a somber veil.

"It's... it's about this afternoon," she breathes out.

"Everything will be fine," I reassure her, squeezing her hand for emphasis. "I'll be with you at the hospital. Every step of the way."

I've done everything I can to divert her thoughts from the impending hospital visit, but it's a colossal task. The afternoon holds a pivotal meeting with my trauma team colleagues. They'll likely reveal the full extent of Natalie's injuries, and the prognosis for her future. Dance is her anchor, Broadway her sanctuary. I can't fathom the devastation if those are ripped away from her.

Natalie twirls a loose thread from the sofa, her gaze far off. When she speaks, her voice is a whisper, barely a ripple in the silence.

"You know, my childhood was... difficult. That's putting it mildly," she begins, pausing to marshal her thoughts. "My parents were always fighting. Home was a battleground, an echo chamber of screams. I'd hide in the closet for hours, hands clamped over my ears, praying for oblivion."

"But look at how far you've come, Natalie," I interject, gesturing to the framed photos of her with Broadway's elite on the wall by the television.

Natalie attempts to smile, but it doesn't reach her beautiful blue eyes. She continues, her voice cracking with vulnerability.

"When I was nine, my dad left. Just packed his bags and walked out, never looking back. I never saw him again. No calls, no letters, nothing," she says, her voice catching on the last words. "I thought things would get better. Without my dad, Mom had no one to argue with, but it got worse. There were men, horrible men. I hated them all."

I simply listen, fingers combing through her hair, planting occasional kisses on her forehead. She manages a small smile, then speaks again.

"That's when I found dance. In the darkest phase of my life, it was my sanctuary. It gave me back everything I put into it. At fourteen, I realized I had talent, a gift, as my teacher would say. I seized the first chance to escape my home. The fear I felt, all of sixteen, journeying alone on a train across the country to New York... If I lose it... if I lose it, my life ends, Rachel. I don't know if I want to keep living," she confesses, tears streaming down her cheeks.

"You've been so brave, worked so hard. But don't say those things, please. I won't leave you, no matter what. I promise."

"I'm broken, Rachel," she admits suddenly. "I've never had a real relationship. They always end badly. I want to blame it on what I saw at home, but maybe it's me. I barely have any friends. In dance, any new person is a potential threat. It's hard to make genuine friendships," she explains, burying her face in my neck.

"You won't be alone anymore. I promise. I'm here, and I'm not going anywhere. You have no idea how stubborn I can be," I reassure her, kissing her knuckles.

And then, words become unnecessary. Her fingers trace lazy patterns on my arm, raising goosebumps in their wake. I stroke her hair, my lips brushing her forehead in a soft whisper. Natalie sighs, curling closer into me, until there's not an inch of space left between us.

Everything else fades away. Time is measured by the rhythm of her breathing and the occasional flutter of her eyelashes against my collarbone.

Whatever happens at the trauma center this afternoon, whatever news awaits us, I won't leave her. It's strange. We've known each other only for a short time, but from the moment I saw her lying on that hospital bed, I knew she was special.

Perhaps one day, all the dreams I whispered to her in the ICU while she was in a coma will become a reality. At least, I'm willing to try with everything I have.

In a few hours, she'll receive one of the most critical news of her life. I hope for the best. If it's not, I'll be there to pick up the pieces, to put her back together with gentle touches and soft words, until her light shines again.

Epilog

A year later.

I'm pacing the theater's wings, restless and wired, my heart thrumming beneath my ribcage. My fingers tremble as they clutch a bouquet of roses, as if the thorny stems could anchor me to some semblance of calm.

The chatter of the audience filters through the heavy curtain, growing louder with each passing moment. I peek through a gap in the crimson fabric, observing a sea of faces that fills the theater, from the elegant boxes above me to the endless rows of burgundy seats below.

The lights begin to dim, and the room falls into a hush. The murmurs of excitement melt away. I tighten my grip on the bouquet, the stem groaning in protest.

And then, Natalie steps onto the stage as the prima ballerina, and the crowd erupts into roaring applause.

My mind is drawn back, unbidden, to the past. The emergency room of Watson Memorial. The woman on that stretcher, her bruised body clinging desperately to life. Her face lit up with joy when she heard the news that her leg was fully healed. No residuals. Never in my wildest dreams did I imagine this moment.

Seeing her here, staking her claim among Broadway's brightest stars, leaves me breathless.

The melancholic notes of the violin accompany her entrance, stirring vivid memories. They're nothing more than echoes of the past now, but those afternoons spent by her side in the ICU are a testament to how far she has come.

One by one, like bricks being removed from a wall, we dismantled her fears and insecurities. Along the way, something beautiful bloomed between us, a real-life version of the fairy tales my grandmother used to read to me at bedtime.

The orchestra's tempo quickens, matching the frenzied beat of my heart. Natalie appears to float on the stage, completely in her element. Her natural expressiveness fills the room, commanding the attention of everyone present.

Her body defies the laws of physics, and my medical training cannot find a rational explanation for her movements. It's pure magic.

The audience watches her, spellbound. Some are on the edge of their seats, but none are more captivated than I am. I want to shout that the woman dancing on stage, moving with the grace of a celestial being, is the same woman who trembles beneath my touch each night.

"She's even better than before the car accident," whispers a young dancer next to me.

Another dancer nods in agreement, her mouth agape as she watches Natalie perform.

"I don't know how she did it. Everyone had written her off. They thought she would never dance again," she adds.

But they don't know Natalie. She was determined to prove them wrong, and she has done so in the most spectacular way possible.

Before I know it, the performance reaches its climax. The audience rises to their feet, and applause fills the auditorium. I wipe away the tears streaming down my cheeks.

Natalie exits the stage amid cheers and stops. She smiles at me as I approach her, her skin slick with sweat. Loose strands of blonde hair stick to her forehead and neck. She's panting despite her extraordinary stamina.

"That was...I can't even find the words...it was perfect," I assure her, wrapping my arms around her neck to kiss her.

When we finally pull apart, her eyes shine with unadulterated joy.

"I had forgotten how incredible it feels to be on stage. I don't know how to thank you, Rachel. You've always believed in me, even when I'd lost all hope," she sobs, tears of joy rolling down her cheeks.

"I'm so incredibly proud of you," I breathe into her ear, my words a hushed echo against the cacophony of applause that surrounds us.

Our embrace is cut short as her fellow dancers swarm her with congratulations. I reluctantly peel myself away from her, stepping back to let her bask in the well-deserved adoration. This is her moment under the spotlight, her moment of hard-earned triumph. We'll have our private celebration later.

"Ready to go?" Her voice breaks through the chatter an hour later, fresh from the shower and donned in casual attire.

Outside, the cool breeze of the New York night grazes our skin, a stark contrast to the heated atmosphere inside the theater. Broadway is alive and pulsing, its energy infectious.

Natalie's gaze lifts upward, her eyes drinking in the neon lights surrounding us. A solitary tear shimmers down her cheek, glinting like a tiny diamond under the streetlights.

To me, the city's never-ending chaos—illuminated skyscrapers, ceaseless noise, a tapestry of languages from tourists—has always been overwhelming. But for Natalie, this cacophony of glaring lights and sounds is home. She wouldn't trade it for the world.

"I will never tire of this," she sighs, her head finding its place on my shoulder. "The lights, the crowds, the raw energy in the air. I've missed it too much."

Our hands intertwine as we navigate our way home, our wedding rings glinting under the neon glow.

"I love you, Rachel Harris. You've made all my dreams come true," she whispers, her grip tightening around my hand.

"And I'll spend every minute of my life making sure they continue to," I vow, my voice carrying the weight of my promise.

Natalie's smile widens at my words. She wraps her arm around my waist, and in that moment, I know that out of the millions of souls inhabiting this city, fate has led me to the one I want to spend the rest of my life with.

New York is a city of dreams. As the lights of Broadway recede in the distance, they're a beacon of hope and promise—a testament to Natalie's tireless journey to reach this point. She may thank me, but she's my inspiration to chase dreams, even when they seem unattainable.

Natalie teaches me that you must keep the flame within you alive even in the darkest hours. She reminds me that love isn't about a single spark, but a million little moments that make it grow day by day.

Beside Natalie, our future shines as brightly as this city that never sleeps.

Other Books by the Same Author

If you liked this book, you'll probably like the following books as well:

Trilogy Watson Memorial Hospital
Interconnected stand-alone books

Doctor Stone: A Sapphic Medical Romance

A decade ago, a tragic surgery forever altered the lives of Dr. Jackie Stone and Sarah Taylor. Haunted by the loss of that patient, Dr. Stone has since immersed herself in her work, believing that if she stays busy, she can escape the pain of her past.

Sarah Taylor, now a determined intern at Manhattan's prestigious Watson Memorial Hospital, finds herself under the supervision of the very doctor who was present during her brother's ill-fated surgery ten years ago.

As she strives to become a renowned surgeon, Sarah must grapple with the emotional weight of working in the same hospital where her brother died, under the watchful eye of the woman who couldn't save him.

Don't miss this riveting sapphic medical romance exploring the intricate dance of forgiveness, healing, and the transformative power of love.

Doctor Torres: A Sapphic Medical Romance

At 27, Nicole Hunt is a rising star in health and wellness, captivating audiences with her dynamic podcast and entertaining TikTok presence. In a special series for Heart Month, she sets her sights on interviewing some of the nation's most prominent medical professionals, including the reclusive

Dr. Inés Torres.

Dr. Torres is a 40-year-old distinguished cardiologist with a reputation as steely as the scalpel she wields. Her life revolves entirely around her work, leaving no room for love or leisure.

As the effervescent Nicole steps into Dr. Torres's strictly regimented world, sparks fly, and an unexpected connection forms between the two women. Can Nicole's warmth and charisma melt Dr. Torres's icy exterior and unlock the door to a new, fulfilling chapter in her life?

Immerse yourself in this captivating sapphic medical romance, a heartwarming journey of love, healing, and the power of letting go.

Doctor Harris: A Sapphic Medical Romance (This book)

Tie Break: A Sapphic Sports Romance

Brooke McKlain is a household name for tennis fans.

Elena has no idea who she is. She just knows she's ruining her life.

When Brooke decides to take a much-needed break at a luxury hotel in Hawaii, she doesn't expect that the woman who challenged her from the very first moment will show her what love is.

Elena will make her question many things, and now love spins onto her court, revealing what she's been missing.

But their worlds are too different, and things are never as easy as they seem... especially when the public image you want to give outweighs your feelings.

A Cup of Love. A Second Chance Sapphic Romance.

Phoenix is about to realize the dream of a lifetime. Her small café in the heart of Edinburgh is ready to open. It's been years in the making, but it's been worth it. The opening is booming, and the café fills up with friends and family.
But when Erin Miller shows up by surprise, it can only mean one thing: trouble.
Why is she back in Edinburgh?
Phoenix doesn't quite remember how she came to be friends with someone like Erin Miller, the high school rebel girl, the same one who broke hearts without thinking about the consequences.
One crazy night, some alcohol and something happened that Phoenix would rather forget forever.
The next day, Erin disappeared...for six long years.
What was she doing now at the opening of her café?

Why did he still feel the same butterflies every time Erin Miller smiled?

She says she's changed.

Is that possible, and can someone like Erin Miller change?

Does she deserve a second chance, or will she disappear again as she did six years ago?

Collins Memorial Hospital is a series of stand-alone lesbian romance books that share some of the characters and workplace.

The books can be read in any order. However, each book offers insights into the characters that can help you delve deeper into the rest of the books in the series.

Books published so far:
- Dr. Park
- Dr. Kumari
- Dr. Wilson

Dr. Park: A Lesbian Medical Romance.

Dr. Laura Park has a promising career as a surgeon ahead of her.

A former child prodigy, she has been educated in one of the best medical schools under the supervision of the prestigious Daniela McKenna.

At the age of twenty-seven, she moved from Boston to Los Angeles in search of a smaller hospital that would allow her to grow faster as a surgeon.

Little did she expect that by a quirk of fate, she would find herself as interim chief of surgery, fighting for the permanent position against much more experienced doctors.

Perhaps it was also destiny that her former teacher showed up in that small hospital one day, awakening old memories but not telling her real reason for being in Los Angeles.

Meet the ambitious Dr. Park, the elegant and enigmatic Daniela McKenna, the cautious Sofia, and the funny

Arya in this lesbian medical romance full of friendship, self-improvement, and maybe a few tears.

Dr. Kumari: A Lesbian Medical Romance

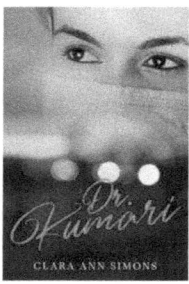

Arya has time for only one thing: saving lives as a surgeon. She is not interested in a relationship. Her life is already too complicated without adding new problems into the mix. Besides, there are too many other women out there to settle for just one.

Patricia wants to be seen as more than a single mother. Her seven-year-old son fills her life, but after leaving behind the toxic relationship with her ex-husband, she's been longing to feel wanted again.

A night out with her friends, a sexy woman at a nightclub, and some alcohol shake up her initial thoughts.

Fortunately, Patricia will never see that woman again.

She didn't even give her a phone number, so her little secret would be safe. After all, Los Angeles is a vast city to cross paths with someone again. A chance meeting is unlikely.

But life is full of twists and turns, and fate is all too capricious. Neither of them expected to see each other again, let alone in a hospital with Patricia's son needing emergency surgery.

Will they be able to ignore the chemistry between them?

Will they give in to their feelings and face their fears and desires together?

Dr. Wilson: A Lesbian Medical Romance

I don't understand why the hospital director has insisted that Siena Collins work in oncology.

She is a spoiled brat, unreliable, and causes too much

trouble in a department where we must look into the eyes of death every day.

To make matters worse, she can't even touch or talk to patients. She is still in medical school and considering quitting altogether.

Her "job" basically consists of bringing coffee, making a few photocopies, and getting in the way. Yeah, I guess her most significant contribution is getting in everyone's way all day.

I wish I could take Arya's advice and tell her to ...

But there's one small problem I forgot to mention: the hospital is named Collins Memorial after her grandfather, and her father is the big boss.

So here I am, trying to save lives while dealing with her immature attitude and tight pants.

That girl will be the end of me...

Nashville. A Lesbian Romance

Sex, drugs, and rock and roll.
Jackie Thomas' life could be summed up in that mythical sentence.
After leaving home at the age of 16, she wandered around the country, making a living in various bands as a singer or guitarist.
Now, at 28, she has risen to the top as the lead singer of the Black Magic, a heavy metal band with a legion of loyal fans.
Mary Crawford is a rising figure in country music. Dubbed by the press as the "Princess of Nashville," she is making her way in a band with her two older sisters under the strict guidance of her father. He conditions every aspect of her musical career and her life.
Sparks fly between them when they must travel to Las Vegas as judges for a talent show. The rock star's strong and irresponsible personality clashes with the good

judgment of the country singer. Still, they soon discover that they have more in common than they first thought. After all, Las Vegas is a city full of magic.

But does what happens in Vegas always stay in Vegas?

YOUNG ADULT SAPPHIC ROMANCE

Liar: A Young Adult "fake date" LGBTQ+ Romance

Nina Álvarez is living the dream.

She's the high school basketball team captain, a social media sensation, and one of the most popular girls at school. But when a misplaced comment goes viral, Nina's future comes crashing down.

With accusations of homophobia threatening to destroy everything she's worked for, Nina devises a daring plan: fake-date Alexia Taylor, a proud and openly gay girl

from her high school

Alexia is her polar opposite. She's a brilliant, introverted aspiring scientist with her sights set on NASA. And she wants nothing to do with Nina's scheme.

However, when Alexia's best friend Cris gets involved, she soon finds herself unable to say no.

As Nina and Alexia play their roles in this high-stakes game of pretend, they find themselves drawn to each other in ways they never expected. Amidst the whirlwind of high school drama, basketball games, and social media scandals, the two girls discover that sometimes, the line between love and lies isn't so clear.

Operation Vanessa

Riley, the high school resident rebel, never thought she'd fall for anyone—especially not Vanessa, the untouchable cheerleading squad captain.

In a world where social expectations and invisible barriers dictate the rules, they are on opposite sides of the high school spectrum.

But love won't be ignored. Overwhelmed by her feelings, Riley turns to Alexia, a straight-A student with a gift for words. Together, they hatch a daring plan inspired by Cyrano de Bergerac to capture the cheerleader's heart.

Milton Keynes UK
Ingram Content Group UK Ltd.
UKHW010640040324
438885UK00001B/175